CHERRY-1
A Combat Controllers Tale

By T.J. Judah

This is a work of fiction. It is not technically or historically correct nor is it intended to be. It is, in short, a romantic adventure thriller. Any reference to persons living or deceased is strictly coincidental.

CHERRY-1 A COMBAT CONTROLLERS TALE

First edition. August 28, 2023.

Copyright © 2023 T.J. Judah.

ISBN: 979-8223799719

Written by T.J. Judah.

Cover art by M. Zimmerman and L. Zimmerman
Collaboration by M.L. Judah

Introduction

The time frame is the early 1970's. RJ is just out of high school when he gets a low draft number. Not willing to take any chances he enlists in the US Airforce. He decides to go for adventure and rapid advancement so he opts for a career field called "Forward Air Controller," or Combat Controller.

While on leave just before his first assignment to SE Asia he's enjoying civilian life for a few days prior to his departure. In a chance encounter at a casual restaurant; he meets a young lady that he spontaneously nicknames, 'Cotton Top' because of her beautiful white hair.

Over the next few days, they fall madly in love with each other. When it's time for him to leave he explains to her that his job will require complete anonymity so they will not be able to communicate while he is deployed.

It just so happens that his lady love is working towards being a nurse. After completing her education she's desperate to find RJ in SE Asia so she enlists in the Airforce as a nurse.

While in the SE Asian theater, she learns in a case of mistaken identity that RJ has been declared KIA (killed in action). Believing he's gone, in a terrible state of grief, she goes underground herself.

Chapter One

It's amazing where your hopes and dreams can take you, until one of them turns into a rolling nightmare.

I had given up hope. This was going to be my last gig. My little Pop Country band and I had traveled the country far and wide for months in search of her, to no avail. I was done. My heart was heavy, and yet. In the back of my mind, I still sensed something good could happen.

When I step out onto the stage of the Speedway in Terra Haute for our final performance. That day will be the end of my search, one way or the other.

We're at our next to last stop at a mall near Boulder. We tuned up the instruments and started to wind up the crowd when out of the corner of my eye I thought I saw a speck of pure white, was it another mirage, or a dream come true? "Play on guys, the audience awaits."

Chapter Two

The year was 1967, I was a sophomore in high school in our small midwestern town. I worked at the local Tack and Feed store stocking, running the register, loading the supplies and all sorts of other chores that go along with a teenager trying to save up for his dream car. I had pictures of her plastered all over the walls of my bedroom, which irritated the rest of the family but, she was me, with four wheels and the aura of an angel.

She was the second generation of the Stingray and was adorned with chrome side pipes, a white convertible top, and shiny mag wheels which totally accented the Cherry red paint job. I woke up in the morning with my eyes full of her essence, and went to bed at night dreaming of the day she would be mine.

I had been working at the Feed store since I was fifteen and as long as I kept my grades up, I could work as many hours as Bob and Larry Fieldstone would let me. Back then minimum wage was about $1.60 an hour and the object of my dreams would run me about $3500, give or take a buck or two. At the rate I was going by the time I graduated high school in '71', I could purchase her outright.

I would need a bunch of additional hours to afford the insurance which was ghastly expensive. With no car payment, I figured I could handle it easily. With the extra hours I could save up for trade school tuition. I wanted to be a technician and work with technology at the local electronics factory. I had heard about some new technology called Lasers that had all sorts of potential for measurement, entertainment and even medical uses. I was eager to explore that field and have been studying up on the concepts.

I got on great with Bob, Larry not so much. As long as I kept the products flowing and the floors clean, we tolerated each other. Secretly I think they liked to play good boss bad boss to keep me on my toes.

At school I studied electronics and ran some track and cross country, skills that would serve me well in the future. My family consisted of my brother Tom, who was a couple years younger, my sister Lanora, who was a couple years older, and Mom and Dad. They ran a restaurant down close to the highway called the Lazy J. It was good for a great home cooked meal. Grandma and Grandpa are retired but helped out at the restaurant, especially for special events like ball games anniversaries, birthdays, and lately, a lot of funerals.

Everyone that knew me knew of my dreams and what I was going to do to make them happen. As well as the energy needed to achieve them. Dad would scold me now and then cautioning me that there was more to life than having a car. It only served to make me more determined.

As it happens, I also like to run. It clears my head and energizes my soul. I'm on the track team this spring and am looking forward to running the mile and two-mile runs. I have a running buddy, Clint. Clint and I have been running the lanes of our small town since grade school. Clint is fast on the short runs; I like the long runs. This week is the state championships and we are super excited as it will be our first time to compete at that level. We have to qualify of course; I think we have times good enough to make it in.

Mom and Dad have supported me on everything I do so when I turned out for sports, they were thrilled I was interested in something other than cars.

The meet came up fast and we had trained hard. Our qualifications were coming up quickly. Clint ran first in the 100-yard dash and 220-yard dash. He made the finals in the 220 but not the 100. My qualification in the mile came up and I ran a respectable five minutes, thirty seconds, not near enough for a placement in the finals. My two-mile wasn't much better.

Clint came in seventh in the finals, not bad for a sophomore. Maybe next year. I would have to keep working on my times over the summer.

Chapter Three

My sophomore year came and went. As I entered my junior year, I became more and more aware of the war in Southeast Asia. The Draft was going strong and it gobbled up some of my friends from school. A couple of them never to be seen or heard of again. I started thinking about what I might need to do to minimize my exposure, but still doing my duty if called upon. Thankfully I still had two years of high school remaining to think it over and hopefully it would end before my future plans are interrupted.

Every day my mom would watch the TV news with concern for her friends' sons and daughters that are involved in the conflict, in some form or fashion, from fighter pilots to nurses to ground pounding Jar Heads.

Every now and then I would see her sobbing at something she had seen on the TV. Now and then she would get a phone call from someone at the Church and she would pray with them over the phone. My dad did quite a few dinners for bereaved families. Way too many.

During my senior year the war was still dragging on. I was busy working my fingers to the bone at the Feed store, and was very nearly my goal. It was looking like I might be able to purchase my Cherry Red Stingray just after Christmas 1971.

She was actually a 1967 model with very few miles on her and was currently in the possession of a friend of mine who due to unforeseen circumstance, could not afford to drive the beauty. She was sitting in his barn under a tarp, well protected from the elements.

I was looking forward to graduation and had lined up some classes at the local Vocational Technical school and was schedule to start in the fall of '71'.

Spring track season was full on and as a senior I had picked up my times considerably. Clint made it to state for the 100- and 220-yard dash medaling in both. I was anxiously waiting as the mile was the premier event of the meet and was the last event. I got off to a decent start and hung back a bit to size up the competition. My best races were when I let the lead guy go out and burn off some energy while I waited to see how strong the field was.

As we rounded the last turn, he was about fifteen feet ahead of me, I waited to see if he was going to kick when he didn't, I zoomed past him. By the time he realized I was in afterburner it was too late. I collected my medal and raced home to celebrate.

Later that spring I picked up my car from Jed the previous owner, and traded him a large stack of one-hundred-dollar bills for the keys and the title. The object of my dreams was now mine forever. I got a special license plate for her, "CHERRY-1."

I fired up the engine and she came to life with a gentle purr. I popped the clutch and the side pipes started singing a tune that was sweet music to my ears. I drove around town and met the family at the Lazy J restaurant for a rousing celebration. With diploma and car title in hand I, "Roy Jansen," or RJ as everyone called me, was ready to take on the world with love and laughter.

Chapter Four

The summer was perfect, the weather was great for a lot of top-down convertible evening drives around town. The car was a veritable "Chick Magnet," I had no shortage of company and really enjoyed this time with my friends and family.

As fall approached, I continued working with Bob and Larry down at the Feed store. I even got a nickel raise to $1.65 an hour. I still had plenty of reasons to work and save as I had my eye on a little bungalow outside of town between the Tech school and the Lazy J restaurant.

I was really getting into the tech school environment. It was a little less tense than high school but more focused on professionalism. High School was mostly a distraction for me. This tech school was serious business.

Mom and Dad had no reason for me to leave home, but I was ready to spread my wings and sprout some interests of my own. There was some new tech coming to the local electronics factory and I had my sights set on learning the skills and knowledge necessary to get that job.

Lasers are the next big thing and I was anxious to get in on the ground floor. I was interested in the many uses that had been developed for the devices. From entertainment to communications to navigation. I was eager and ready to learn.

Everything was going according to plan and was working out great. I was a few weeks into the fall semester when life took a turn and everything suddenly changed. I came home from work one afternoon and the atmosphere was extremely tense. I came into the living room and found my mom sobbing uncontrollably. My dad was trying to console her but there was nothing he could do but hold her. Lanora was nearby and she was shaking with dread. Tom was just pale and trembling. My first thought was, "Oh my God who died?" They all looked at me and shuddered.

I noticed that Mom was holding a piece of paper, it was the new draft lottery numbers. It turned out I had a very low number and my number could literally be called any day now. The paper was wet with her tears by the time I got a chance to look at it. I hugged her and held her for the longest time and told her, "It will be ok. I know the Lord Jesus as my personal savior and I trust him to protect me."

As I studied the paper my knees buckled, I sunk to the floor, my breath escaped me. My number could be up any day, the war was suddenly face front and ugly.

After I caught my breath and gathered myself, I looked up at dad and said, "What am I going to do?"

He handed me the phone book and said, "Go to the nearest Airforce recruiter and sign up as fast as that cherry red fire breathing monster can get you there."

I collected my high school diploma and headed to the Airforce recruiter's office in a neighboring town. He was very glad to see me for some odd reason. Ah, he didn't get many Airforce recruits in his district, I was the first one he'd seen in weeks. Well, I told him "I'm here now and I need to get ahead of this draft lottery number." He understood and sat me down to take the required tests. After that I had to get a physical. Assuming all was clear I was going to be on the next flight to San Antonio for Basic training. I had been studying electronics and was physically fit due to my work at the feed store.

I passed the tests easily and after parking my car in mom and dad's garage with a tarp over her. I packed a small bag and caught a bus to the induction center in a nearby city. That was a very long day. It started with a six o'clock roll call, then another physical, injections for flu and other assorted diseases. And then we waited. The room was large and there were probably three hundred souls in attendance.

We were divided into groups based on what branch of service we were going into. Myself and about ten others were going into the Airforce. A few were going in the Navy. A couple of guys were going to the Coast Guard. The rest of the guys there had been drafted into the Army.

About three o'clock or so a uniformed man entered the room and hollered out to listen up. If your name is called you are now a Marine. He began listing off names and guys started running for the doors which were blocked by armed Marines. Guys were screaming and crying and rolling around on the floor.

Personally, I was absolutely terrified he could still call my name, I've never been so scared in my life. Turns out he was only calling out the names of draftees.

Basic training was tough, but manageable. I really enjoyed the rifle qualifications and the confidence course. One day we had to pull some details outside of town at a different base. A group of us had to clear tall grass from the roadways. We were whacking away at the grass when one of my northeastern squad mates stumbled into a nest of scorpions. Hundreds of them scurried about clearing the area of Airforce trainees.

Next, we got to do a few days of KP, that's kitchen police in one of the officer's mess halls. I actually enjoyed it, since being around food preparation at the Lazy J peeling potatoes was a breeze.

I made it through Basic Training ok with an overall Excellent grade. Which gave me a choice of future assignments.

I wanted to be a tail gunner on a B-52 Bomber, but alas I was turned down because I was too tall. The rapid advancement was what I was interested in. Turns out they were getting shot down pretty frequently due to swarms of missiles over enemy territory.

So, I moved on to the next interesting career field. Combat Controller or FAC (forward air controller) looked interesting, it also promised rapid advancement. I was accepted into the training program. Which was a combination of field work and electronics.

The electronics consisted of various radios UHF VHF HF, (ultra, very, and high frequency) both use and repair. It also included instrument landing systems that are portable. They are brand new to the field with the latest digital technology; as well as a short course on ATC (air traffic control).

I trained on the equipment and various aircraft at Hurlburt field in Florida. It was almost like being on a beach vacation. O-1's, O-2', OV-10 Broncos, A1-E's, A-26's, and various gunships from C-47's to C-130's. It was a lot to take in.

My new roommate Steve, was from Northern Michigan, he was training on some cushy admin job. He was a slob and thought he was quite a ladies' man. I mostly tolerated him but he was also good company, for a narcissistic person. Kind of like hanging around the class clown, very full of himself.

One day after school was out, we decided to hit the beach. I had warned him repeatedly that he needed to keep his clothes off the floor. He ignored me of course.

I kept all my belongings hung up and put away securely, I even put socks over the top of my boots. Scorpions, which are native to the area were known to drop down off the ceiling and land who knows where. I didn't want to find one in my boot. He laughed at me for being so uptight. I got the last laugh however.

He dug through the pile of clothes on the floor and found his swim trunks. Suddenly he started dancing around like a maniac. He yanked at his swim trunks and out popped a you guessed it. A small pale looking scorpion about two inches long.

"Oh my God," he screamed, "what is that?"

Wasting no opportunity I said, "You are doomed man, done for, kaput. Even if we got you to the hospital in time there's no antidote."

He stood there and sobbed for a minute while I collected the specimen and disposed of it.

I let him go on like that for a couple more minutes.

"Dude, it didn't even sting you. If it had you would be smarting in physical not emotional pain. You are actually darn lucky."

He cussed me for a few minutes and low and behold, he cleaned up his pile of clothes. Then we hit the beach.

The whole training experience was fascinating to me. The tech is really what attracted me to this career field, and the advancement opportunities. That is, until reality set in.

One day after my duty day was done, I came back to the barracks and was about to turn in for the evening. I opened the barracks door and the hallway was full of guys clamoring about collecting their gear. There was an airman standing outside my door waiting. I asked him, "What's all this?"

He replied, "gunship crew getting ready for a night mission."

"Wow," I said, "What's your job?"

He had a solemn look on his face and serious mood.

"I lay prone on the open ramp door and call out rockets."

I paused for a second; looked at him and said something weird like, "Well, have a good one."

Hurlburt was a huge training base with a lot going on. Every now and then you could get a dose of someone else's reality.

My reality was about to take a more serious turn as well. We arrived at Howard AFB in the Canal Zone of Panama during the rainy season for the field side of training. It was hot and sticky, did I say, it was HOT and STICKY.

The equipment did not work well in the humidity, I did not work well in the humidity. I was also living with the biggest ugliest bugs I had ever seen in my life. Did I really volunteer for this? Oh wow, there's a sloth living in the tree outside my barracks window.

After settling in our housing, the next thing I know we were strapping into a C-130 tactical transport plane and nervously readied ourselves for the next stage of training. These folks wasted no time.

Tonight, we get to jump out of a perfectly good airplane into the deepest darkest jungles of Central America. Yes, the very same place where zillions of people died building the Panama Canal.

The squad leader screamed out, "Time to suck it up buttercups, this party is just getting started."

We lined up at the jump door, hooked our chutes to the lines. Suddenly the green light blasted in our faces and we were whisked off into the nothingness of the night. After conking my head on the side of the plane I spent the next few seconds both dazed and terrified, and then very peaceful, as we drifted down to a barely lit landing zone.

The ground zoomed up to meet me as I crumpled into a pile. My equipment and my body landed with the force of a linebacker's tackle. As I was trying to collect my thoughts and my stuff, the squad leader materialized out of nowhere and started barking orders as if we were in mortal combat.

"RJ, get your stuff and set up the Glideslope and the infrared equipment for the LZ (landing zone). Choppers coming in pronto and they need to know where to go. Come on get with it." He hissed at me in a viperous tone which I swear anyone within earshot could have heard and understood.

I set up the short-range glideslope transmitter and the laser locater beacon and got them running. In the flash of an eye the choppers loaded with Army Rangers came barreling out of the sky. The roaring wind from the rotor blades was ferocious.

Rangers poured out of the choppers and charged down the LZ for their jungle training exercises. We boarded the choppers for the return journey as our job was done. The Rangers had to find their way back to base through the densest jungle I had ever seen. It would take some of them weeks to trek the three miles back to base.

The next phase of training was orbiting in a small single engine airplane called an O-1 (observation). We would call in targets or downed airmen for close air support and rescue helicopters. Other times we would use an O-2 airplane to put a team down on a potential LZ and set up locater equipment for the transports to drop supplies or reinforcements.

The squad leader harped constantly that you fight and work as you train so get with it...very loudly. I thought we were doing ok but that was far from the truth; according to the NCO (noncommissioned officer) in charge. The CO (commissioned officer) in charge had nothing good to say...ever.

Panama was not a place to be trifled with. There were all sorts of wild life and other things to pay attention too. I went downtown with a group of guys on a day off. It was a really different world for me. We walked around and took in a few sights. We traveled over to one of the other Air Bases on the other side of the Canal where I found a great deal on a good SLR camera. On the way back to base I noticed two guys walking around in police looking uniforms. One of guys I was with said, "Those guys are secret police the Le Guardia, stay away from them and never travel alone off base."

A few days later one of my roommates came up missing. He asked me if I wanted to go to town with him and I politely declined. He went anyway. Weeks later they found him in a hole in some ratty prison. Starved and eaten by bugs he has lost over fifty pounds. His only crime was being alone. They sent him back to the states and we never saw him again.

I was taking in some fresh air and saw a guy pop out of the back door of the Security Police building. Humm, I thought, I recognize that guy. He was asking me a few days ago if I wanted to party. I asked him, "What do you mean party?"

He said, "You know smoke some pot." I replied, "Are you nuts they will hang you buy your ankles if you get caught. No thanks."

I watched the guy walk across the lawn and uh oh, he was meeting with one of my new roommates. They chatted briefly and off they went.

Later that day I confronted my new roommate and I asked him. "You know that guy you met with is an SP, right?!"

He laughed and said, "Yeah I know but he's super cool."

That evening I was catching up on some reading, about to turn in. My new roommate grabbed his shower stuff and went down the hall to the showers. A few minutes later there was a knock on the door. I got up and answered it. I opened the door and I counted no less than ten Security Policemen. Taken aback a bit I stammered out, "Can I help you?"

"Is so and so in?"

"Nope, he's in the showers."

They collected his stuff and we never saw him again either.

The last day of training came and the CO handed us our orders and our next stripe.

"Congratulations" he said, "RJ, I wish you well and a successful career and safe return home. You have done well and have upped the standards for Combat Controller training. Your use of infrared and lasers has upped our game considerably. Well done and good luck." My new call sign was of course, "CHERRY-1."

Chapter Five

Training was over. My squad mates and myself waved goodbye to Howard AB and the steamy jungles of Panama. We transitioned to a holding station where we waited for our final orders to be cut. We would eventually join up with a group of Army specialists to form teams to do actual Combat Controller functions. In the meantime, we got two weeks leave before shoving off to the SE Asian theater of operations.

I flew to the closest town from my home with an airport, then took the bus home. I had been cautioned before departing to wear civilian clothes and to never speak of our job, rank, mission or destination to anyone, including family.

Obviously, my family knew I was in the Airforce, but that was all I could tell them. In fact, I was told to tell them that I would be completely out of touch for the next 16 months. I would have a general P.O. Box number where they could send mail, however I could not respond. The integrity of our mission and our personal safety hinged on total secrecy.

My family met me at the bus station where there were hugs and kisses all around. I was really glad to see everyone and catch-up with the latest news.

My sister Lanora was getting married soon. My brother Tom was about to graduate from high school. He was teasing an interest in aviation and was taking flying lessons at the Vocational Tech school on weekends. The restaurant was booming as usual, and the Feed store missed me greatly. I heard Clint, my running buddy from high school was drafted and was in Army training.

As you might have guessed, after a wonderful home cooked meal down at the Lazy J. My thoughts turned to that Cherry Red fire breathing monster I called; my CHERRY-1. I pulled back the tarp, dusted off the upholstery, charged the battery, and turned the key in the ignition.

She roared to life and purred like the kitten, I mean, the hungry mountain lion that she was. I drove off down the highway to blow out the cobwebs. I was getting hungry again by this time so I stopped at a fast-food restaurant in a neighboring town to grab a quick burger.

Just as I got out of the car a little sedan pulled up across from me and a young lady hopped out and rushed for the door. I popped off, "Hey what's the rush Cotton Top?"

I noticed that she had the most beautiful natural white hair, I couldn't resist the urge to say something. Out of the clear blue, it hit me to call her, 'Cotton Top.'

She turned around and gave me a side glance and said, "I was just trying to beat you inside." She struggled for a moment to find something else quippy to say back to me. She finally said, "What happened to your hair?"

I followed her up to the counter and waited for her to order. I told the clerk I would get it. She protested for a second but relented after I said, "You can pay me back by having a civil conversation with me over dinner." She kind of sneered at me for a second but surrendered and we sat down for a soda, burger and fries. I gushed over the meal as it had been quite a while since I had experienced that type of meal.

She wondered out loud, "Well where have been that you haven't had a burger for so long?"

"I've been out of the country on business. It was really hot and humid there so I cut off my hair to stay cool.

I said, "Do you have a name other than Cotton Top?" Which I affectionately called her one more time."

"My name is Cherry."

I just about fell out of my chair. I'm sure the surprise was written all over my face which caused her to quip.

"Is there something wrong with that!"

I stressed fondly, "Oh no, not even a little bit. I actually love it completely. My Name is Roy, you can call me RJ. When we leave, I've got something to show you."

I listened intently as she described how she was going to nursing school and working at a local clothing store. Her family was from the east coast and the distance was hard on her sometimes. She was coping by staying busy with school and work.

I watched her mouth move and her eyes blink, the expressions change on her face, and fell deeply and madly in love with her. Cotton Top was going to be my bride someday.

After finishing our meal, we went outside, as we walked up to the cars, I said. "Cherry, meet Cherry."

I walked her around to the back of the car to get a gander at the license plate. Her eyes glistened and she wiped away some spontaneous tears. I couldn't help myself; I leaned in and gave her a gentle kiss on the cheek. She whirled around and planted a great big kiss right on my lips and wrapped her arms around me with a huge hug.

Indeed, a moment to remember, one that's going to keep me going in the tough times ahead.

Chapter Six

Cherry Wilson, aka Cotton Top, and myself grew very close over the next few days. We sampled most of the decent restaurants in town. We soon traveled over to my home town for a meal, and introductions at the Lazy J. My folks fell in love with her almost as fast as I did.

My mom pulled me over and asked me, "What are your intentions with her?"

I told her, "Look, we're having a great time right now. I haven't told her yet what the next few months are going to be like. I've got a lot of thinking to do and one thing for sure. I hope and pray we can get back together when it's over."

Mom said, "You better be straight with her son, she's the best thing I've ever seen around you."

"I will mom. Believe me the last day is going to be an insane level of torture for both of us."

Later that week we went to the park over by the High School. It had a nice little pond with some swings and picnic tables. I parked the car and turned on the radio, we got out and walked slowly around the pond.

We returned to the car and listened to the music. As we swayed gently in each other's arms, I sang the Unchained Melody softly in her ear. I held her close and could feel her heart beat. I could also sense that she knew this wonderful time was almost over. Hopefully it was not done, just over for now.

We sat down at one of the tables and I pulled out the title to the 'Cherry-1.'

"Cherry, I want you to take care of her till I get back. Will you do that? I trust you more than anyone to take care of her and it's also my commitment to come back to you as soon as humanly possible."

The tears dripped steadily from her beautiful blue eyes as she silently shook her head in agreement. I choked back the heaviest emotions I had ever felt as I handed her the keys. We then set off for the bus station.

"Oh wow, I almost forgot, I need a snap shot of you two Cherry's together."

I explained to her that my next few months are going to be a blackout of information. I had a general mail address she could write too, but I could not write back. Everything was going to be censored by the government anyway to protect my identity, location, and any mission particulars.

"All I can tell you is that I'm in the Airforce."

We hugged until the station master crowed that my bus was leaving NOW. I touched her fingers as I stepped up in the door.

The driver said, "Oh, how touching, come on dude get on the bus already."

I took my seat and watched her as long as I could, my eyes glistened as she disappeared slowly into a speck. Her white hair shinning in the evening sun as we rounded the turn for the interstate. Please Lord Jesus, bring us back together safe and healthy as soon as possible...Amen.

Chapter Seven

The airplane landed with a thud and taxied toward an open hangar. I saw my squad collecting their baggage and equipment into a pile in the middle of the floor. I joined them with my stuff as well. Inspectors went through every stitch of clothing, bag, and file to make sure we weren't keeping anything compromising.

I was sure I didn't have anything to worry about as I had been very careful. Suddenly I remembered, I had completely forgot about the negatives in my camera. I began to sweat for a minute, but they moved on, and we loaded quietly into a C-141 transport for parts unknown.

The journey was long and tiring. All I knew for sure was we're heading west by the way the sun moved around. We landed at Hickam field in Hawaii for refueling and food. We were able to stretch our legs for a bit and then it was back into the air. We next stopped at Clark Field in the Philippines. Same thing, stretch, food and refuel.

We landed one last time in South Vietnam at Da Nang AB. We unloaded and went to our quarters to temporarily house us, and our equipment. After catching up on some sleep the CO rounded us up for a briefing.

"Grab those maps over there, Staff Seargent Jansen," barked the CO.

He pointed to a spot on the map that looked way out in the middle of nowhere. "This is where team Baker is going for the next few days. You will chopper in and set up for some air drops by C-123's and 130's. They are not going to land, just swoop down, pop the drag chutes, drop their loads and get out of there. This LZ is not big enough for takeoffs and landings.

However, they still need us to help them find the location, get in and out, without incident. The future of this location is unknown to us, suffice it to say heavy equipment and Marines are likely to soon follow.

Study the nav maps and memorize the comm frequency, take as little paper and other evidence of your presence as possible. You're going to be ghosts for the next few months gentlemen. I hope you all have your wills and life insurance paperwork up to date, because as simple as this op sounds, there are no guarantees. If you're praying men now is a good time to speak to your higher power."

I muttered under my breath, "I never stop."

"Go to the armory and check out side arms and rifles, good luck and God speed gentlemen. Expect to be in the field for a week or more. Team Alpha your turn is coming up tomorrow."

Well, I thought. The fun is about to begin. We trotted over to the armory and checked out our weapons, checked the ammo and secured them for the trip ahead. The chopper was warming up on the helipad as we scrambled aboard.

The pilot asked, "Who's in charge of this op?" The Master Sergeant next to me squeezed his shoulder to let him know it was him. He was the experienced man for this otherwise green team. It was myself, Staff Sergeant Jansen, Army Sergeant Wallace, and Master Sergeant Ballard. The pilot and Sergeant Ballard exchanged some hand signals and we lifted off, soon we were skimming the tree tops at high speed. You didn't want to fall out of this thing. You would be mincemeat in an instant.

I followed our progress on the Navigation map and checked off the way points as we passed over. After about an hour we circled around what appeared to be a deserted bare spot in the forest. It had been defoliated recently and dead vegetation was all over the ground. We landed and immediately set up our equipment. Wallace on the radios, Ballard on ATC duties and myself working Glideslope and Location Beacon equipment. Everything was up and running when out of nowhere, Aircraft started buzzing around like locusts.

Guided by Sergeant Ballard, one by one they swooped in and dropped their loads. Equipment piled up at the end of the LZ, soon after, choppers full of Marines dropped out of the sky and disembarked quickly from their vehicles.

Their leaders gathered around and conferenced. They were on a search and destroy mission. We were to wait there until they finished their mission and or needed immediate rescue operations. The Marines collected the material from the airdrops and disappeared into the forest. We monitored the comms to arrange for close air support from gunships or fighter bombers if needed.

It seemed to be a pretty routine mission. At the end of the day the Marines started straggling back to the LZ, tired but otherwise unscathed. One private needed to be medevacked out after stumbling over a bungee stick. We got a chopper in and out for him fairly quick. It looked like he was going to be ok.

Darkness closed in around us, the Marines set up a perimeter and we settled in for the night. There was absolutely no sound, it seemed even the leaves on the trees were silent. I drifted off to sleep when suddenly the "Pop...Pop...Pop" of small arms fire started sounding off in the distance.

Everyone was suddenly wide awake and at full attention. Some of the Marines had night vision equipment and scanned feverously for any signs of enemy activity. The noise died down just as quickly as it started. Few of us fell back asleep.

Morning came and we opened cans of rations for a light breakfast. The radio crackled to life and orders started flowing in rapidly.

"Enemy movement had been detected about five klicks away to the south of your location. Movement is northward towards you."

The Marine Lieutenant came over to us and requested immediate evac. Ballard called in for a full evac of the platoon. The radio crackled back after a few minutes delay.

"Request denied, stand and hold your position. All choppers are deployed elsewhere. It will be at least two days before we can get to you."

"Well, that was disappointing," whispered the Lieutenant. "Orders are orders," he pulled all the NCO's together, "get everyone ready for a stand. We're going to be here for a while."

The day dragged on with no further obvious enemy activity. The sun was setting and the bugs started flying around, circling like vultures. We dug in for the evening and waited anxiously for any more enemy activity.

Ballard said, "This is a fairly normal op. There might be some probing later on in the night. They like to get your attention and scare you; it makes you over tired, which then makes you dull headed the next day. So, grab some sleep as soon as you can and conserve your water. We will get out of here in two days or so."

It was way past midnight, there was a nervous quiet. Suddenly the radio crackled to life, instantly getting our attention. It was hard to focus for a minute due to the constant sleep interruptions.

The voice on the other end said, "There's a large enemy force at least platoon strength about five hundred yards to your south. Alert everyone to be still. A gunship is orbiting just over you; I need you to flash some infrared signals to highlight your position."

I did some morse signaling with an infrared light stick. About a minute later the sky erupted with a lightning storm of tracers. The gunship chopped at the ground with mini guns and 20-millimeter canon blazing. A couple of 105-millimeter canon rounds caromed off the forest walls. It ran on for about five minutes.

The Lieutenant whispered to Ballard and Wallace, "They were using us as bait."

Wallace whispered back, "Well I hoped they bagged their game. That was too close for comfort."

About an hour later the radio came back to life and gave the all clear. I think I shook myself to sleep. I woke at dawn and fired up the nav equipment for the choppers to come in. We choppered out of there in two hours on our way back to Da Nang.

Ballard leaned over to me and told me, "This was a fairly routine op. Only one injury and it was minor. This may not be the case much longer as the President is escalating the B-52 heavy bombing campaign over the North trying to get them to the negotiation table. Which is going to mean more pilots and crews shot down and more ops for us to find them and arrange close air and rescue. When we get back burn the maps and codes along with anything you wrote down. We leave no evidence of our ops."

All I knew was I was dirty, bug eaten, and tired. I'm checking my weapons in and hitting the shower, grabbing some hot chow, and sleeping for a week.

That week lasted about 24 hours and then it seemed like all hell broke loose.

Wallace stormed into the quarters and started banging on my bunk, "Get up man, we're on for an emergency op."

I collected myself and got over to the briefing room. The CO was handing out assignments like a mad man on steroids.

"The Buffs (B-52 heavy bomber's) have taken major damage; several are down from the DMZ (de militarized zone) to the Gulf. We might even have to sneak past the border to facilitate a rescue. You're with Wallace today, Jansen. We're putting as many teams out as we can."

By the end of 1971 the mission parameters for the controllers had shifted from ground to Air due to difficulty getting in and out of ground locations, unreliable equipment and the lack of available FAC Controllers.

I was briefed on my target for the day and instead of a chopper to drop me in, I boarded an O-1 single engine prop plane. We are going to spot targets on the trail. The bean counters had figured that the North was completely out of trucks, but supplies and combatants were still flowing in remarkable numbers.

"Hey," I said to the pilot. "How's it going today?"

"Hi, name is Lt. Gary Baker, it's going up and around and around today. Same as yesterday and the day before that."

"Anything unusual about today's mission," I asked.

"No," he paused. "Except today we're going in deeper down the trail, there might be some hostility, we're going to need to mark targets for the fast movers."

"Fast movers," I said, "what's that?"

"Jets, and high-speed prop planes, A1's, OV-10's and the like." Baker replied.

"Any friendlies in the area," I asked.

"Not that I know of. Buckle up, the air is rough today."

We buzzed the target area while fast movers circled above waiting on coordinates and visual markers. Just when we were about to turn back, I spotted something unusual in the trees. A smoke chimney that had no visible activity around it. Indicating that there was activity close by.

"Cherry-1 to all available resources, target is at the following coordinates, visual marker to follow." We dropped smoke in a path along the intended target line and made for home. "Cherry-1, target is marked, good hunting. Cherry-1 out."

We headed back to base and refueled waiting around just in case we were needed to spot downed flyers; the pilot kept the motor running. Sure, enough one of the fighter bombers had been shot down in the same area we had just come from.

We took off, this time we searched for a downed pilot or crew. We buzzed the area looking for any sign of the pilot. They had ELTs, emergency locator transmitters, and smoke to mark their locations. They would pop smoke when they heard us in the area.

We started to hear the ELT pinging in the headset and then spotted a smoke plume.

"Cherry-1 to rescue Aircraft, downed airman at the following coordinates smoke to follow. Looks like a small LZ close by, no hostiles observed in the area. Cherry-1 out."

We circled nearby waiting for the Jolly Green (chopper) to reel them in.

"Great job everyone, crackled over the radio, thanks."

We started for home when we heard a loud pop coming from the left wing. Fluid started pouring from the hole. Gary frantically switched the fuel from the left side tank to the right as we watched the fuel gage start to plummet toward zero.

"Wow" he said, "this is going to get interesting." He screamed into the mic, "Mark our coordinates and send a mayday, we're going down."

"This is Cherry-1... Cherry-1 anyone on this frequency, we are going down at the following coordinates, marking the location with smoke."

"Roger Cherry-1, this is Da Nang base, all resources are otherwise employed, you're on your own for now. Base out."

Lt. Baker found a small clearing about three klicks away from a small village.

"Sure, hope they're friendly," said Gary.

The engine went quiet as we drifted down to earth. Gary was one of many highly skilled brave and accomplished flyers of the O-1, and other FAC aircraft.

We bumped into the ground and took a quick assessment of the area. Sensing no immediate threats, we hopped out and started processing a solution for the problem.

Gary motioned towards our right side and said, "I saw a small village that way about three klicks. I'm going to go see if I can get some gas, hopefully enough to get us out of here. You stand guard by the plane, make sure it stays intact."

Gary took off down the trail. I found a spot where I could see all around. Suddenly all alone in a foreign country, my thoughts soon turned to 'Cotton Top,' my girlfriend Cherry, my motor car Cherry, and home. I hoped they were all ok and living their best lives.

I prayed every day for all of us to have the best lives possible with the Lord Jesus's love and protection.

Chapter Eight

"Hello Martha," said Cherry. "How are you, she asked?"

"I'm fine dear, I just wanted to come and check on you and selfishly on my part, to see if you had heard anything at all from Roy."

"Well Martha, as you know he told us all he would be in a blackout, and so far, that's been true. I've heard nothing. That doesn't mean to say that I don't try watching the news and sending the occasional letter to his drop box. Unfortunately, I get most of them back as the military is censoring his correspondence. I've got the feeling that if I say anything that might distract him from his mission priorities, it gets scrubbed."

"I've experienced the same thing," said Martha. "I just worry so about him. I know he's a big boy and can take care of himself but I see the most awful things on TV. If we only had a word or two, at least something letting us know he's alive."

Cherry said, "I'm graduating from Nursing school at the end of the month and I plan to join the Airforce as a Nurse and I'm requesting to be stationed in the South East Asian theater of operations. I will do my duty, I also plan to search for him, at least some news of him on my days off."

"Oh, that sounds awfully dangerous Cherry," said Martha. "At the same time incredibly brave. Of course, you will let us know of anything you find out."

"Yes, I will and you do the same for me. Good day Martha, I wish us all the very best."

Martha drove the car home, her eyes glistening with sadness and worry. Arriving there, she parked the car and went inside where everyone was waiting.

Dan asked her. "Has Cherry heard anything...anything at all." He questioned.

Martha replied with a shrug of her shoulders. "No Dan, she has not. She is however determined to find out something about him. Even going to the lengths of joining the Airforce as a nurse and requesting posting to SE Asia."

There was a collective gasp among the gathering.

Tom was about finished with twin engine pilot training and with the end of the draft, he was looking at becoming a commercial pilot.

Lanora is married and expecting her first child with husband Daren. The grandparents are still healthy and going strong helping out at the Lazy J.

They had both good news celebrations with Soldiers, Sailors, Marines, Coast Guardsman, and Airmen coming home, and still, other news with funerals since the fighting was still raging on.

It was the summer of '72' and there was talk of a cease fire. Everyone was eagerly awaiting news of that. The President had reauthorized heavy bombing of the North with Operation "Rolling Thunder." Our losses were accumulating as well.

Everyone resumed their lives while awaiting any news of RJ. There was none for the foreseeable future. The end of his assignment was just a few months away.

"Surely we will hear something soon," muttered Martha as she prepared the evenings dinner.

Cherry had accomplished her goal of a Nursing degree. With that diploma in hand, she went down to the recruiter's office to enlist. She rumbled up in the Stingray, got out and opened the door to be met by Chuck, the Airforce recruiter for that district.

"Haven't I seen that car before," he quizzed.

"Likely you have, it belongs to RJ, I am in custody of it until his joyful return."

"Ok then, what can I do for you young lady," he asked.

"I'm here to enlist as a nurse and I want to be assigned to SE Asia."

"Well, it seems both you and I have hit the jackpot today. You get what you want and I fulfil my quota. And a nurse gets premium bonus points for me."

Cherry filled out all the necessary paperwork, passed her physical, swore in, and requested to drive to the coast instead of flying. She was temporarily assigned to Travis AFB in California for in-processing. Within the month she was ordered to Saigon for duty.

Cherry-1, the car, was parked in the impound lot at Travis with a tarp over her to conceal her identity.

Cherry settled in after the long and arduous journey. Taking her position as a Ward nurse, she watched and listened intently for any sign of RJ. Even staking out the mail room where his P.O. Box was located. She had to be careful to not attract any unwanted attention.

One day while working the ward one of the patients noticed her name tag. "Say...your name's Cherry?"

"Yes, it is Airman."

"I've heard tell of an FAC (forward air controller) that goes by the call sign Cherry-1. In fact, he and his crew saved my life, and the lives of many others while spotting for downed aircrew."

Her face turned as white as her hair. "Have you heard anything about where he is and if he's still alive?"

"No ma'am I haven't, they keep his identity and location top secret. I've been in here for some weeks now and my information sources are pretty old. I'll reach out to my buddies at NKP Thailand to see if they've heard anything. Last I heard he was spotting out of OV-10's for the A-1 Sky Raiders' and A-26 Invaders' that were doing close air support for downed aircrew.

I would be very careful ma'am seeking out too much intel on him. Someone might mistake you for an enemy agent. Cherry-1 is very effective at his job. There are many an enemy that would like to eliminate him or at least find out everything he knows. By the way this conversation never happened ... do you understand!"

Cherry was flooded with emotions. Any news was incredible on its face. Should she take a chance and write to Martha? Maybe not. It would likely get quarantined and censored.

She waited anxiously for any news the airman in the hospital ward could give her. She checked back with him a few days later, he was gone having returned to duty. He did leave her with a note in her mail box in the office.

She read the note, three little words, "he is alive." She let out a gasp.

She addressed an envelope to the Lazy J in the USA. In it was the handwritten note.

"He is alive."

Chapter Nine

Lt. Baker trotted off down the trail to the village. He moved carefully so as not to attract the wrong kind of attention. Arriving at the outskirts of the village he spied a couple of things that might contain gasoline. There was an old tractor and a couple of long boats in the river for fishing.

He spotted a container large enough to hold gas to get them out of there. As he approached the container an elderly Vietnamese man came out of a hut waving his arms and frantically speaking some French and presumably asking him, "What are you doing?"

Gary tried to communicate, not knowing French, it was difficult. He was finally able to get it across that he needed fuel.

The old man smiled and pointed to a gas pump near the boat dock along with a couple of five-gallon tins. Gary offered him money which he refused. He wanted the knife strapped to his belt.

"It's a deal," gushed Gary.

The old man even added in a little cart to tote the gas back to the plane.

I saw him coming down the trail. The sun was setting, it was getting difficult to see around us. Gary pulled up with his precious cargo, unscrewed the fuel cap and started to siphon the gas into the wing tank. Hopefully this is high enough octane to get us out of here, he thought to himself.

"I hope this stuff is good enough to fly on." Gary said. "We're going to try anyway."

"I'm with you man," I told him.

"Help me finish this up and stow the cart out of sight. When you're done go out there and see if you can figure out which way the wind is blowing, we need all the help we can get getting this thing in the air."

"Right on man," I told him as I sprinted out into the middle of the field. "Looks like about a ten mile an hour south wind."

"That's great," he said, "it will help get this little bird into the air."

He climbed in the pilot seat and cranked the engine. It sputtered for a few seconds and then roared to life. I pushed the small plane into take off position and climbed in.

"Buckle up RJ," Gary said, "this could get interesting."

I quickly complied and he pushed the throttle forward. By this time, it was pretty dark so I got out my 'Star Scope' and scanned the ridge to the east of us for any activity. The scope lite up light a Christmas tree. I tested the radio.

"Cherry-1 calling base, Cherry-1 calling base. Requesting a fire mission at the following coordinates. Multiple bogeys traveling slowly along the ridge. We're running short of fuel so will be unable to paint the target with laser."

"Where the hell have you been Cherry-1!" Belched the voice on the radio. "Transmission acknowledged, assets on the way. Get on home."

"Roger base, it's a good story. I'll tell you when we get home. Cherry-1 out."

The rest of the flight was routine. Gary landed the plane and we debriefed in the Ops center. The mechanics had the plane ready by the next morning.

Chapter Ten

Due to massive increases in aircraft mission activity and a shortage of FAC's, I was challenged nearly every day for one mission after another. Sometimes flying out of Da Nang, sometimes out of NKP Thailand. I spotted from various aircraft including O-1's, O-2's, and OV-10 Bronco's. The O-1's was getting shot down frequently because they're slow. The mission parameters have been changed to the faster aircraft.

That didn't mean they didn't get shot down either, but it was harder for the ground fire to hit them. Some FAC's were even spotting out of jets. A few times I manned the night scope in the Specter's, C-130 gunships filled with many resources to put on the ground.

We were notified of intelligence that there was a buildup of enemy activity near Cam Ranh Bay Airbase. For several nights in a row, we orbited the area searching for any signs of activity. There were a few hits on the Star Scope but nothing substantial was to be seen.

We set down at the Airbase for fuel and food and maybe catch some sleep. I was teamed with Pilot Captain Lee Colson and Sergeant Wallace for the time being. The Cam Ranh Bay buildup was seemingly a dud.

We went over to the NCO club for dinner and listened to a pop band play for a while. It was getting dark and late buy this time. Wallace and I walked over to the Base hotel to catch some sleep. Captain Colson went and made sure the plane was ready for another night mission.

I had just fallen asleep when somebody came screaming into the room.

"Zips in the Wire, Zips in the Wire, get up and grab your gear and get over to the tower to call in coordinates."

Wallace and I jumped up and ran the fasted mile I had ever run to get to the tower. We climbed the tower steps just as the first rockets started hitting the far end of the base. I made it up the ladder and fired up the Star Scope and started calling out coordinates to Wallace who was calling them in for artillery strikes and Gunship strafing runs.

The enemy had dug a tunnel under the base fortifications and were pouring out onto the field. They had overrun some of the revetments where the aircraft were stored. I saw our OV-10 go up in flames along with a couple of F-104's. Artillery was starting to walk them back and a flurry of Gunship activity sent them flying.

The Marines set up a perimeter and were standing their ground. Rockets continued walking closer and closer to our location in the tower. I was calling in air strikes as fast as I could identify them. I was finally able to see where the rockets were coming from and called in my final set of coordinates just as the last of the rockets hit just a few feet away.

Suddenly I head the cracking of wood and the straining of metal as the tower we were in started coming down. I felt myself falling and then I must have hit my head.

I don't know how long it was before we were pulled out of the wreckage. I kept passing out and was soaked with blood. I called out to Wallace but never heard anything back.

I started to come too, my eyes were covered with bandages, everything was blurry and my head was swimming. In my delirium I actually thought I saw Cherry for just a moment and then I passed out again.

I laid there for days and slowly I got my sight back and was able to sit up. I scanned around for anyone I knew. I found out that Wallace didn't make it. Captain Colson survived but he was on his way back home.

An attendant came by and asked me if I would like to walk around. I said, "I will try."

We walked a few steps and I staggered a bit but regained myself and we walked over to what was left of the chow hall. I sat down for a lite meal when one of the Base Commanders came over and introduced himself.

"Hi, I'm Colonel Bass, you guys saved our bacon the other night. Sorry about your buddy. Sergeant Wallace, I believe? On the plus side the prettiest nurse I've ever seen came by to see you a few times. You were out of it. Too bad, she acted like she knew you from somewhere. She had to get back to Da Nang. Get well Sergeant Jansen, we need you up in the air as soon as possible. And by the way, get those Dog Tags back where they belong, ok."

It was September '72' and the Buffs are at it nonstop. FAC's are struggling to keep up with all the mission essentials, from spotting ground targets to arranging close air for downed aircrew. Occasionally an FAC would contribute to a rescue operation manning the winch in the Jolly Greens or even roping down to assist injured aircrew or soldiers on the ground.

Suddenly mid-October the President announced a cease fire and then next thing we knew many of our Airframe assets were transferred to the South for their continued use. The US is deescalating and 'US' personnel are starting to head back to the states.

Mine, and the remaining FAC's presence was still required, there are many aircrews still unaccounted for after "Rolling Thunder" was complete. We went out day and night scanning for any sign of them.

Our efforts are rewarded often with grateful aircrew anxious to get home themselves. Slowly over the next few weeks the frequency of finds was less and less. I confess I was ready for a rest.

I collected my stuff at base NKP Thailand and flew to Saigon. I had not checked my mail box at the Embassy in quite a while. I expected it to be full of letters from home and of course 'Cotton Top.'

I opened the box and stuff fell out on the floor. There were dozens of letters from home and many from Cherry. The ones from Cherry are heavily redacted which made them very hard to read. Hello how are you, love you, I am well, bye. The military sure knew how to carve up a nice letter. Soon I would be able to write them back.

I rotated to an R&R location for debriefing and rest. They checked me into a hospital to make sure I didn't have any rotten diseases. I was a bit malnourished and dehydrated. The bugs had done a number on my otherwise gorgeous complexion and I needed a haircut.

I took advantage of the time to write letters, play ping pong and shoot pool. I swam in the swimming pool, and one day I stumbled onto an old guitar stashed in an equipment closet. As I strummed the guitar, the vibration of the strings calmed by stressed and shaky nerves. I hadn't noticed how shaky I was until I tried writing letters. It was hard and painful at first. After a few days of massive IVs of fluids and Steak dinners, the shaking started to calm down.

Playing the guitar really calmed my mind, my nerves, and soothed my spirit. After a while I got good enough to play some actual songs. Some of the guys and myself started up a little music group. It was a lot of fun and a great way to pass the time.

After a few weeks I was transferred to a hospital in the Philippines for final testing to ensure I had no communicable diseases that took time to manifest.

I continued my guitar playing, even buying one of my own, a sweet looking twelve string made of, you guessed it, Cherry wood.

Letters went out but nothing was coming back in. Apparently, I was still a security risk.

After clearing that last hurdle, I received orders to go to Howard AB in Panama to be an FAC instructor. I would spend the rest of my enlistment doing that duty.

I heard through the grapevine that Lt. Gary, the O-1 pilot with whom I spent many a mission, was alive and well and was going to be stationed at Howard AB as well. It will be great to see him.

Who I really need to see is Cherry!

Chapter Eleven

"I heard that RJ was flying out of Da Nang most of the time. So, I'm requesting a transfer to the hospital there." Cherry told the administrator.

He said, "Are you sure? There's no guarantee you will find him there. They keep those FAC people under lock and key."

"I'm going to try. If that's all I can do, then I've done something."

The transfer was approved so I went to Da Nang AB. I immediately started asking around for any information.

Nobody and I mean nobody would have anything to do with me. Until one evening at dinner a man walked by and slipped a note under my tray.

I pocketed the note and hurriedly finished my dinner. I went outside and opened the note.

It read, meet me in the admin office of the hospital at 2100 hours. Tell no one and destroy this note immediately.

I complied and waited nervously until time to meet. I cautiously made my way over to the office and went in. A uniformed man sat across the desk.

"Hello," he said, "my name is Master Seargent Ballard. I flew with RJ in the early days. I will have to tell you; you are even more stunning than he described. If he wasn't working mission central, he was talking about you and that silly car. Honestly, he started sounding like a beating drum. It was quite clear he loves you very much."

"Where is he, how is he," I stammered out.

"I can only tell you that as of yesterday he was just fine. He's flying out of NKP Thailand right now, spotting for the 'close air' folks. They may work him to death. FAC's are in high demand and short supply. It would be a miracle if you were to find and meet up with him. The military keeps those guys under wraps to protect them, you and your families from foreign agents.

In fact, this meeting never happened, do you understand Cherry?"

"I understand, sir, good day."

I went back to my Quarters and buried my face in my pillow sobbing. The tears are both for joy and sadness.

The days wore on, I did my duty at the hospital. It was a normal duty day when the room was filled with people scrambling to gather everything they could. I watched for a moment and asked someone, "what is going on?"

"There's been a rocket attack and violent incursion with many deaths and injuries at Cam Ranh Bay Airbase. We're collecting everything we can as the medical staff and hospital were hit as well. In fact, grab a go bag you're coming too."

I collected my stuff and boarded a chopper for the ride over to Cam Ranh Bay. As we approached the airbase the devastation was significant. Aircraft burned on the runway, barracks burned and buildings blown to pieces. We landed and set up a triage as fast as we could. The deceased were placed in body bags and were being flown out to the states. The wounded and injured were being brought in on stretchers.

We treated them as quickly as possible. The worst ones were flown out to Saigon or Da Nang. There was a lot of noise beside us as crews were trying dismantle a tower that had crashed down. There were reports of survivors in the wreckage. They worked frantically to get them out.

After things settled down and everyone was accounted for, I strolled through the tents to see if I could help. There was one airman who was unidentified, his uniform had been torn off in the course of getting him out of the tower wreckage. His ID and papers were not with him either, no Dog Tags either.

Just then I noticed his auburn hair and a small birthmark on the back of his neck. Oh my God it was RJ. I hovered over him as long as they would let me. I finally had to leave and get back to Da Nang.

At last check he was alive and moving around. The doctors said he was going to be ok.

Back at Da Nang I went back to the same routine. For weeks I never heard anything else until one day in October '72' I was walking by the Air Operations center and someone was talking about an OV-10 blown out of the sky.

"Call sign Cherry-1... was KIA."

I dropped to my knees and sobbed for what seemed like hours. I immediately went to the admin and requested a transfer to Australia. I was going to work at a hospital there working with burn victims. A place where hopefully, I can do some good.

I spent the next months working with them. It was difficult but rewarding work. I put RJ, aka Cherry-1, on a shelf and moved on. My heart was broken, maybe helping others will somehow help it mend.

Chapter Twelve

Right before I rotated out of the Philippines, I got a call from Master Sergeant Ballard. "Hey RJ, this is Ballard."

"Hey Sarge how's it going?"

"I'm fine, about to rotate back to the States."

"To what do I owe the pleasure of the call?"

"Well, I wish it was good news, but it's not. A few months ago, a young nurse showed up at the hospital in Da Nang. She had the most beautiful white hair."

"Oh my God, was it Cherry?"

"You guessed it man. It was her. She searched for any intel on you and of course I was not able to give her much. You were still flying out of NKP. I gave her what I could and she accepted that with grace and continued working at the hospital.

One day she was walking out by Air Operations when she overheard a conversation talking about a downed FAC call sign...Cherry-1."

"Oh no, well that was obviously a mistake."

"Yes, but she didn't hear the correction, it was actually China-1. Devastating for that guy and his people but clearly not you.

She never heard the rest of the story and immediately requested a transfer. Her orders are confidential just as yours are. She thinks you're a dead man. I don't know how to fix this. Only that God you're so fond of can fix this one my man. Good luck, Ballard out."

Just as the letters from home and Cherry stopped, I was able to start writing back. I would be able to spend a few days at home before rotating to Panama.

Chapter Thirteen

Home, what a sight for sore eyes. I dropped my stuff on the floor of the Lazy J and sat down hard on a bench. I was exhausted. Noone had noticed me yet till a new young server wandered over and asked me.

"Can I take your order sir?"

"You sure can, a cup of coffee and a burger and fries. Where is everybody?" I asked.

"Oh ... they're all at home waiting for RJ to come home."

"I laughed and said, glad to meet you."

"Oh my God" she exclaimed; "they will be so excited."

"They will be fine for a little while, how about that burger, I'm starved."

She scurried off and relayed my order to the cook.

He hollered out, "Yes ma'am, coming right up."

I heard her squealing into the telephone. I figured I would get invaded any minute now. I still needed that burger pronto.

The whole bunch showed up roaring in with a cloud of dust. They exclaimed in delight as they rushed the room.

Dad said, "Stand up man I want to measure you."

I stood up and hugs all around. Mom was crying and Tom and Lanora are beaming from ear to ear.

"How are you RJ," asked Dad.

"I'm physically fine, but I'm sad to say I've been mistakenly reported as KIA, poor Cherry thinks I'm dead.

Mom said, "I wondered why her letters stopped coming."

"Did she tell you where she was, or what was going on?"

"No, nothing. I expect she is grieving your loss and is not dealing with it very well."

"I understand, I'm not dealing with her loss well either. Let's celebrate what we have today. I can work the other problems tomorrow."

We partied late into the night, catching up on a years' worth of events. I could only tell them that I was alive, had a lot of work to do, and was heading for Panama to finish out my enlistment. And, "Oh by the way, I've learned to play the guitar."

I hung out for a while with some old friends from school. I went down to the Feed store and hung out with Bob and Larry for a while as well. They are all doing fine and glad to see me. I was glad to see them too, not much had changed. In a small way it was comforting.

I asked about Clint my friend from high school. Well, it turned out he was drafted into the Army and they discovered he was an extremely fast runner. They put him on the Army track team. He's been running all over the country competing in track meets representing the Army. Who'd a thunk that out.

I went over to the neighboring town where I had met Cherry. I went to the Nursing school and checked in with the admin to see if they had heard from her. The last time they knew of her she was in Saigon at the hospital there. That was very old news.

The time passed quickly and I took the bus back to base to rotate to Howard AB.

It was the same Howard as it used to be, only quieter. The number of trainees has dwindled to nothing as the Vietnam situation was winding down and the military was changing the FAC program with new technology.

However, there was still a trickle of new people and they were just a bit different from previous trainees a little more laid back I would say.

I was unpleasantly used to Howard AB and the local area, fortunately it was the dry season, not quite as sticky. The Canal Zone was a lot like a coastal city in California, there was a few fun things to do, most of all, there was a Library with a fax machine.

I just about burned the thing up sending faxes all over the country searching for any news about Cherry.

Once in a while I would help the guys on the flight line doing some avionics maintenance. One day I was helping the Radar guys on a C-130 quick turnaround. The C-130's are used to transport all sorts of cargo and people to Central and South America. Mostly Embassy runs taking bags of mail and other supplies. One day they even used a C-130 to transport a package the size of a tissue box. Mind boggling.

So, I was helping the Radar guy tune an ADF, (automatic direction finder) a World War II relic that had to be tuned from the flight deck all the way to the back behind the wheel wells. It took at least two people to handle it and you had to run headsets and cables and all sorts of paraphernalia to get it done right.

Done right was an absolute because in this area of the world the ADF and the Search Radar are the only navigation devices that work consistently.

I'm running back and forth and the clock is ticking on us. All of sudden this guy, dressed in a business style Airforce uniform comes up and starts asking us questions. When he questioned me, I told him he would have to check with Ops to find out any information on the Aircraft and its cargo and destination. He checked out the name on my uniform and wandered away, asking the same questions of the other guys working on the plane.

A couple days later we were all summoned to the Commanders office and given a reprimand for a security violation. It seems we are supposed to commandeer that guy and hold him for the SPs as a Security Test. That guy was really tricky, but I got the last laugh.

About a week later I was sitting in the Flight deck of a C-130 doing daytime testing on a recently repaired HF radio (High Frequency). Day time testing was required because the HF did not work at night in the Panamanian geographic region due to the atmospherics at night.

All of sudden I see this guy pop out of a door next to the Ops building. I recognized that guy instantly. He didn't notice me in the flight deck of the C-130 and walked right in front of the plane on his way to mess with some other maintenance guys working down the flight line. Everyone is supposed to display their IDs prominently for anyone to see.

I watched him walk all the way over to the other Aircraft and start to question the guys. That's when I called the Tower.

"Aircraft Tail Number 62618 calling Howard Tower."

"Tower to 62618, state your business."

"There's a security violation at ramp location B-21. I repeat B-21. There is a guy dressed in an Airforce Uniform with no ID harassing the maintenance guys."

"Transmission acknowledged 62618, SPs on the way."

I sat there and waited for the SPs to show up. They came roaring up with sirens and lights blazing, armed personnel jumped out of the vehicles, grabbed the guy and planted him on the ground, handcuffed him and drug him away. I laughed till I cried.

Speaking of daytime HF testing. A brand spanking new maintenance Lieutenant showed up one night. The Radio tech working the flight line that night was also new.

I was in the maintenance office waiting to clear the Aircraft off of the Job Board. The process drug on and on. Finally, I caught a ride out to the Aircraft and climbed up to the flight deck where everyone was gathered.

The Lieutenant was giving the techs holly heck.

"Nobody and I mean nobody is going home until I can see that this HF radio is positively working, got it."

I told him. "Lieutenant the HF will not send out voice modulation at night due to the atmospherics here. You have to test the HF during the day."

"I don't care, nobody is leaving until I can hear that radio work."

I spoke. "What if I can show you the radio is working?"

"What do you mean," he asked.

"There are some neon fuses in the maintenance office. I will go get them and we can string them along the top of the Aircraft, if they light up when you key the mic, then you can say the radio is working. How about it?"

"Go get the fuses."

I drove back to the office and collected a box of neon fuses, don't know what they are there for or where they came from, but I was going to put them to good use. I sure hope this works.

I went back to the Aircraft and gave the fuses to the Crew Chief. He spread them out from nose to tail. The E model of the C-130 has a long line antenna that runs the length of the Aircraft. He stepped back in and we crowded around the top hatch, I told the Radio tech to key the mic. Those fuses light up like a Christmas tree.

"Satisfied?"

We all went home and caught midnight chow at the dining hall. All's well that ends well, or so they say.

The next night there was another quick turnaround that needed fixing in the middle of the night. This time it was a Radar Altimeter. Radar Altimeters are used in low level drop missions and could be quirky if they are flying over wet lands or water. It would give false readings.

The plane had a write up so I helped the flight line technicians with troubleshooting. The problem is, the receiver transmitter has to be removed and bench checked, repaired if necessary and replaced, since there are no replacement units in stock.

It was a very dark night; the unit was located on the belly of the aircraft. The panel had about eighty so odd pop screws. One twist and they were loose but they stayed connected to the panel, which was nice since it was dark, and I was laying on the tarmac in the middle of the night. Somebody hates me, I just know it.

I popped all the screws and traveled into the shop and bench checked the unit, which was perfectly ok. I ran it back out to the airplane and got back under the belly. Holding your arms up and reconnecting the eighty or so odd pop screws was absolute agony.

I finished up and climbed up to the flight deck where the crew chief was sitting. His eyes got as big as saucers as I entered the cabin. He jumped back and pointed at my shoulders. There are two of the biggest uglies bugs on my shoulders that I, and anyone else for that matter had ever seen.

I jumped back nearly falling out of the airplane while swiping at the bugs. I collected myself and retested the Radar Altimeter as best you could on the ground, signed off the paperwork and went for breakfast, hoping I could hold it down.

Occasionally I had to do my other job. We are using O-2's, it was a push pull twin engine aircraft used for spotter training. The mission parameters had changed since the last time I was here, we spent most of the time doing air to ground spotter training. There was a field of targets spread out in the local jungle, we would use 'Star Scopes' at night and drop flares or paint the target for a helicopter gunship to shoot training rounds at the targets.

On off days, when I wasn't at the library sending and receiving faxes, I spent a lot of time in the gym playing racket ball with a couple of Security Police.

"Say RJ, you're in that spotter program, right?"

"Yeah, what of it," I replied.

"Well, we're curious if you could use that fancy equipment to spot some drug traffickers we've been dealing with. They've been incredibly illusive weaving in and out of the jungle on their way to waiting Sea Planes on the coast. We know it's happening but we can't connect the dots with our limited abilities. What do you say, can it be done and could you do it? We've heard you have some night vision equipment that can spot a cat from a mile up."

"Let me think about, I'll have to get authorization from headquarters. I'll get back to you by the end of the week. It's your serve, hit the ball already."

I began processing the possibilities in my head. This could actually be a great training exercise in some real-life scenarios. Could also benefit the Security Police mission. Drugs in Panama is like soda pop in any US town.

I acquired the required permission from Headquarters and started procuring the resources necessary to do an adequate job. I let my SP friends know we are a go. Now all we need is a schedule and a briefing on mission parameters.

The next day I was in the dining hall having breakfast when this three-stripper sat down in front of me.

"Hey man have you heard?"

"Heard what, my man."

"This place is abuzz with rumors that there is a new and actual mission going to happen around here. Coolest thing to happen in forever man."

"Ok man...where on earth did you hear that?"

"Oh, it's all over everywhere. I also heard that the legendary 'Cherry-1' is the lead FAC. Heard tell they're bringing him in from the states to run the show."

"Wow man, that is so fascinating, why are you so excited about it?"

"Oh well, I'm going to fly as a trainee for the first few missions, then I'm going to take over the lead seat. For this mission I will be manning an additional 'Star Scope' to train on the use of the equipment."

"Who are you exactly," I quizzed?

"I am Sergeant Lackey, fresh in off the boat, so to speak. Apparently, Headquarters is so excited about this op that it's generated a whole new crop of recruits."

"Oh, goody gum drops, this ought to be riot," I said.

Privately my head was spinning, we don't have the equipment or personnel for this level of mission. This should be interesting.

"So have you seen this 'Cherry-1' character?" he said, "I heard he's like a twenty-one-year-old Senior Master Sergeant with a chest full of eye candy."

"I'm not sure," I said, "when is he supposed to arrive?"

"Well, I heard he will be on the next flight in from the States, C-130's brings in supplies and personnel once a week. We should see him come in tomorrow."

"I will be very excited to meet him. I hope he's all that and a bag of chips."

"What's your name man," he asked?

"Oh, well hi I'm RJ, you can call me Cherry-1." Of course, he really already knew that.

Lt. Gary was our pilot for tonight's mission, he and I walked and talked as we made our way to the flight line.

Gary said, "What do you make of this Lackey fellow, seems kind of creepy to me. He really doesn't fit any picture I have of this situation."

"I agree," said RJ. "Bears keeping an eye out. Not sure what to look for though. I think I will sit back seat today and watch what he's doing."

We loaded the equipment for the nights op. Seargent Lackey was spot on and ready to go.

"Careful man," I said, "that equipment is sort of fragile."

He seemed in a lot of ways to be the typical new guy, all nervous and bumbling about. Kind of reminded me of me a few years ago. The O-2 zoomed into the night sky.

We began orbiting in circles moving from one grid position to another all the while communicating with the SPs on the ground ready to interdict anything we spotted.

After about an hour we got a tingle on the 'Star Scope' and then we got a good-sized hit. I called in the coordinates to the SPs. They wanted us to go in for a closer look to make sure it wasn't a bunch of monkeys.

"No, it's not monkeys, unless they can drive trucks."

All of a sudden, I realized Lackey was painting the ground with a laser in the direction of the ground contact. That was about the same time the 'Star Scope' blew up in my face with the flare light from an RPG rocket. Aimed straight at us.

"I screamed into the mic, rocket starboard side."

Gary banked hard left just as the rocket detonated.

The rocket exploded close enough to shatter the control surfaces. We're going down. The radios dead, all the electronics shot. Gary was injured and the new guy, Seargent Lackey was dead. I was ok for the moment, but that could change any second as we are about to hit the jungle canopy. I quickly assessed our location as best I could in the dark, with no instruments.

We crunched into the canopy and the wings sheared off. The impact took some of the momentum off of the downward spiral. After the crunching and crashing finished up. I checked myself out and determined I was still ok. Gary was struggling to breath as there was a huge bruise on his chest from hitting the yoke.

That's when I saw the foam coming out of Lackeys mouth. He had no visible injuries; did he just kill himself?

I looked down and around and discovered that we were about ten feet off the surface of the jungle floor. I pawed through the jumble of equipment to find whatever survival gear and first aid kits I could muster. The plane creaked and groaned as it teetered, as if it was telling us it wanted to finish the journey to the ground.

I questioned myself, are we better off staying put, or getting out of the plane and finding the ground? It didn't matter as the plane slowly nosedived the last few feet into the ground.

After the plane finally settled, I started asking other questions. Did the drug running people know we were up there or did they just get lucky. Do all drug running people travel with RPG rockets?

One way or the other the security of this op was highly suspicious. I hate to think like this but, was this whole op a setup to get rid of me, us?

I would have several days to consider the possibilities as we struggled to find our way to civilization.

Meanwhile back at Headquarters they had reported us downed and considered MIA or likely KIA, that's missing and presumed dead. Once again, I was a dead man. My folks received the visit from the Chaplain and were of course, devastated. Filled with questions they were told it was likely a training accident.

We gathered ourselves and got away from the plane should it catch fire. Gary was in a bad way struggling to breath. It was of course very dark with vegetation surrounding us. I got him as comfortable as I could and started hacking around us with a machete to make us some space.

I cut down some bamboo, laid it down, and lashed the poles together with some webbing from the airplane. Some old boy scout training kicked in and I made him a drag litter.

I made a further assessment of his injuries to make sure he wasn't going to be further injured by traveling. After checking him out I made him as comfortable as possible and we settled in for the night.

I dozed off a couple of times but any little noise sent me into fight mode. I was well armed with both our hand guns and a rifle. I could fight off an attacker if I saw it or them first. I was well aware that I was not invincible.

Gary was struggling to breath so I tried to lift him up and prop something under the litter to hold him there. I looked around for something and actually found an old Army Ranger pack frame. It worked perfectly. He was able to rest for a while. I was anxious for daylight.

The sun peaked through the canopy with shafts of light just enough for me to survey the area more thoroughly. I managed to find an old trail the Rangers used to find their way back to base from their jungle survival training. At best it took most of them at least three weeks to find their way back to base and they were healthy. This could take us months to find our way back.

We were able to travel a few hundred yards a day through the dense jungle even with the ready-made trails. Lt. Gary probably has a collapsed lung, we made some, but very little progress.

Thankfully we stumbled onto some old trails the Rangers had used in their training exercises. We even had ready-made camp sites. I had to do some hacking with a machete but our progress was really only limited by how far Gary could travel in his condition. We had many encounters with Jungle wild life. Most of them I scared off with a loud whistle, a couple needed some extra persuasion. The most relentless enemy was bugs, I hate bugs.

I was able to snare some critters for a protein meal. I had tools to start a fire, we were able to heat and eat a small meal. We still had some of our survival provisions but not knowing how long this was going to take I needed to make use of the resources around us. I'm not sure how good a monkey tastes but it may come down to that.

Gary was looking a little better and was able to sit up and eat his food and drink water. This was a very good thing as he was starting to look a bit malnourished.

I spotted a jaguar circling us. It was keeping its distance but still stalking. There were several kinds of monkeys that harassed us, some of them seemed to want to keep us company. The jaguar's eyes glowed in the dark. The dark was creepy enough but those eyes were like hot coals staring at us. I couldn't tell if it was just curious or hungry. The fire at night kept him away for now. I don't know when the rainy season starts. That might be the end of our night time fires.

We had traveled by my estimation about one and half miles. We needed to pick up the pace. I was able to move a bit more quickly as Gary could handle the jostling around somewhat better. I was trucking along pretty good when suddenly there was a loud bang behind me. I spun around. Gary was sitting there with the rifle in his hands and the stalking jaguar lying dead about fifteen feet away. I had to take a quick break to get my heart back down out of my throat.

We heard planes circling above, presumably looking for us. It was impossible to see us through the canopy during the day. At night we put out such a small heat signature that they couldn't tell us from the wildlife. I learned later this actually turned out to be a good thing. Can you imagine?

Our rations are running out, we gathered water from the daily rain showers. I had lost about fifteen pounds by now and Gary looked absolutely emaciated.

We needed to find food, shelter and transportation soon, if either one of us was going to survive.

I think it was somewhere around day thirty-five when we came across a small river. It looked navigable so I started whacking at the bamboo, after a tussle with the bugs and snakes and other associated critters, I built us a make shift raft. My prayers are slowly being answered.

What a new day brings.

We floated down river for two days and nights. At night we anchored in the middle of the river as snakes are likely to drop out of the trees. I've already had enough surprises to last a life time.

The next morning, we came around a bend in the river and low and behold there was a small village on the river's edge. I navigated to the docks and motioned to the locals nearby that we needed help. I had picked up a little Spanish while I was there, but I wasn't sure what language these people spoke.

They appeared to be hospitable, they gave us some food and rudimentary medical care for Gary. After about a week he could communicate again. We had a brief conversation about our current set of circumstances.

"So, hey man," said Gary. "How do you think we got into this mess?"

"Well, I have my suspicions but it seems awfully convenient that we just happened to be where the bad guys were. Could have just been drug runners that didn't want to be found. The Lackey fellow committing suicide was a bit odd."

"I think a lot about home and what I miss most, Gary mumbled. I miss my wife, Sandra, my dog Rex, hamburgers, a bed, a toilet, TV, newspapers. Even football, I used to love to watch the Dallas Cowboys on TV, even got to go to a game one time. What about you Jansen?" he quizzed.

"Well, you know about 'Cotton Top,' my 'pet' name for Cherry."

"Oh, so that's how you ended up with the call sign Cherry-1."

"Well, I also have a cherry red stingray parked somewhere in the United States of America. I gave it to Cherry for safe keeping and also to show my love and commitment to her. I should've asked the girl to marry me before I left, but I was afraid of what might happen to me. It sure would have saved a lot of the heartache that we've both been through in the past year. At least it would have been a different type of heartache, if something had happened.

Last time I heard she was in Da Nang and misheard a message that Cherry-1 was downed, but later on it turned out to be mistaken for China-1. She never got the correct message. I don't know where she is now. I've been faxing every hospital I can think of trying to find her.

Anyway, I miss all the things you mentioned except I was kind of fond of the Chiefs."

"What are you going to do when we get back to base?" asked Gary.

"I'm going to find out what the heck happened to us. Something very strange happened and I plan to get to the bottom of it."

While the indigenous peoples looked after Lt. Baker, I searched for anything to use to call out, or ride out. I was finally able to ascertain that there was a bus going to Panama City once a month, it had just left right before we got here. Looks like we're going to get to spend some time with the locals until then.

We got into the fishing business and helped out with that food processing, their way. They had some livestock, cows, chickens, goats, the usual farm animals. We needed to be useful to them in return for their good will, we obviously needed to stay there for a while. Best be good citizens.

I learned how to milk a cow and a goat. Gary helped out with some sheet metal projects they needed to protect their domiciles. Gary, (Lt. Baker) was good with technical stuff and even strung some wire for electric lights.

I went back to fishing. Wiring and sheet metal are not my thing. I could however spot a snake in the grass fifty feet away, that came in handy a couple of times. We are still in the jungle after all.

In the evenings we sat around a camp fire, eating smoked fish and roots for dinner. There was very little conversation besides a few grunts and uggs. The two of us weren't completely ignorant of human nature and easily picked up on the nonverbal cues between the Chief guy and his mate, wife or whatever their relationship was. If she was happy, he was usually happy too.

We worked hard not to get on her bad side. Overall, we faired pretty well. We both even gained back a couple of pounds. Still stunk to high heaven. Occasionally it would rain and we would run and get what passed for soap. We still stunk, but we had a slightly more mellow fragrance.

They ate a lot of bugs, big beetles, a lot like the rice bugs in Thailand. The people over there would catch those things, bite the end off and suck the guts out. The kids would harvest the beasts and sell them for a Bot apiece, thus the name 'Bot Bugs.' These folks here seemed to favor boiling them. I will be fishing for my dinner, if that's ok.

Myself and the Chiefs son got to be pretty good fishing buddies. They had cane poles and some nets they strung across the river. The river would rise and fall a bit during the rainy season. Had to watch out for that. The occasional crocodile would float by, we left them undisturbed.

After all the dampness I think I started to get a case of jungle foot. Or something like that. Spent way too much time with wet feet. Every other day or so I would take my boots off and dry my socks by the fire.

I won't miss this experience when it's over, but I will treasure the moments I had with the son and his father 'the Chief' while fishing. I won't miss the bugs and the snakes, one darn bit. That's all I've got to say on that.

I used to go camping and fishing back home, this, is a whole other level.

"My God this is tough." I told Gary. "It's a good thing we're young and strong, I can't even imagine having to do this as a twenty-five-year-old."

"What are you, twenty-two," he laughed.

"Yeah, but I'm about done in. Three more years old, I wouldn't have lasted three weeks out here. In the wilderness, alone, without my guitar. I do miss my guitar too, you know."

"I've heard you caterwauling on that thing, you call that music?"

"Yes, it's my version of Country Pop Rock and Blues."

Gary quipped, "It sounds mostly blueish to me with a side of crack pot."

I laughed out loud, "Hey, I've heard you swooning away on that harmonica of yours. We could make quite the team together, Country Blues Rock with RJ on twelve string and Gary on harmonica. I bet our music would bring tears to their eyes."

"They would have tears in their eyes alright, tears of PAIN." He laughed.

By the time the Bus comes back Gary should be able to travel. I questioned the Chief.

"How long is the ride to Panama City, time, how long, drive, trip, how long?"

"Oh, it's about an hour or so." Chuckled the Chief.

"What, you could speak English all this time?"

"Sure." Said the Chief. "The Rangers used to come through here quite often. I would have sent you hiking the last three miles weeks ago, except Lt. Gary was not ready to travel. If you had been here any longer though, I was going to have to move you guys' down wind, you really stink"

"Well, I'll be, I hope we didn't embarrass ourselves"

He chuckled. "No son, you guys are actually a lot of fun to have around. The Rangers always act like a bunch of tough guys. You two are a bit of fresh air for once. We will actually miss you when you're gone."

"I have a question Chief? How do you keep the mosquitoes away from here?"

"Bug spray," he chuckled, "I have a deal with the Rangers. About once a month they bring me a case of bug spray in exchange for fresh fish and snake skin for their boots. Oh...by the way I'm not the chief, she is' motioning towards his wife. You can call me Alex."

"Well Alex," I said. "You are full of surprises. Next thing I know you're going to tell me you have a college degree or something."

"Oh...well, you guessed right on that one. I have a business degree from university. I really like the business around here the best though."

Hum...Snake Skin Rangers...that might make a cool name for a band.

It turns out the Bus ride to town really was only about an hour away, and that was mostly because of all the stops for people to load and unload their livestock. Holy cow, we were only about three miles away from the base.

We said our goodbyes to Alex and the Chief and the little tribe that had helped us. We boarded the bus along with other local tribes' people and their goats, chickens, ducks, and I think there might have even been a pig.

The Panamanian buses are quite colorful and a lot like riding around in a cattle trailer. They are very nice people though and very accommodating, especially since we looked and smelled absolutely horrible. Imagine the grubbiest hobo you've ever seen and multiply it by ten or maybe twenty. We basically stunk so bad even our fellow riders noticed.

We departed the bus at a stop right in front of the gate at Ft. Kobbe, the army base right next to Howard AB. You had to go through Ft. Kobbe to get to Howard. We got out and started walking toward the sentry.

"Halt," he shouted. "Who goes there?"

Of course, we looked a mess and our flight suits were torn to pieces.

I said, "I'm Senior Master Sergeant Roy Jansen and this is 1st Lieutenant Gary Baker."

And thus started the next level mashup. Apparently, we had been declared dead, and if anyone showed up using our names, they were likely impersonating us.

I sternly looked the sentry in the eye and said, "We're not impersonating anyone, we're personating ourselves. Got it!"

He still refused us entry. Following his orders, I expect. However, we're growing weary of this phase of the adventure.

"Look Private, we're tired and hungry and worn slick. We've been in the jungle for months, let's get this done. Call Commander Phillips First Air FAC training division at Howard, he can verify who we are."

The sentry dialed the phone and said our names and ranks into the phone, "Hey there's two guys here at the gate claiming to be Senior Master Sergeant Roy Jansen and 1st Lieutenant Gary Baker can you verify their identity?"

I could literally hear him screaming over the phone, "OH MY GOD, they're supposed to be dead. Arrest them, they are imposters."

So, they hauled us off to the brig. Well, at least we could get a shower.

The next day a buttoned up looking admin guy showed up and claimed to be our lawyer.

I asked him, "What do we need a lawyer for?"

"You're going to have to verify who you say you are; the real individuals haven't been seen for over two months."

"Really, I said, "Won't our military IDs and Dog Tags suffice?"

I had managed to protect them from the elements in my survival bag. A little tattered but intact.

"No," he said. "You could have likely stolen them from the aircraft wreckage."

"Look, I realize we don't look like ourselves, but it is us. We have several ways to prove our identities. We have passwords on computers, finger prints, voice prints on file at Headquarters. Just check a few of them and we are good to go."

He wandered away and after a few hours he came back and took us to a conference room.

"Ok, I was able to verify the data that you gave me. You are who you are, but there's another problem. You're supposed to BE DEAD."

"What the devil does that mean?" said Gary quite sternly.

Doug the lawyer started coughing up some pretty startling information. "The night mission with the SPs was a setup. Sergeant Lackey was a foreign agent as well as the SPs. Your immediate superior was also a foreign agent.

The goal was to shoot you out of the sky and make it look like a hit from some drug cartel guys. It was actually in retaliation for some clandestine mission both of you were on in Vietnam. You apparently trashed a powerful black market Asian Drug Lord's supply train; he was incensed over it.

He managed to put together intel and figured who you guys are, Cherry-1 and company have quite the reputation. Commander Phillips tipped his hand yesterday; he was their main operative. He has been arrested by the CIA (central intelligence agency). He and his cohorts will disappear.

We need for you to stay put for a few days to made sure we root out any other foreign operatives. You're going to remain dead for the foreseeable future to ensure safety for you and your families."

"Oh well" I said, "I've been dead before." Except this time, it's going to be just a bit different. "We do however, need our belongings."

"They will be over soon from storage, that will be under the cover of darkness."

I didn't want anyone to know that the camera was my prized possession, more importantly, the film inside it.

The CIA was going after the East Asian Drug Lord. Reportedly he was quite the piece of work. Trafficked in everything from drugs to weapons to people. His organization moved around a lot of money and local authorities looked the other way most of the time. Apparently, Lt. Gary and myself dropped a load of lead on his operation and he wanted retribution.

In the meantime, we're getting new identities. My new name is Clay Ledbetter and I'm no longer in the Airforce.

Chapter Fourteen

RJ, aka Clay thought, my new identity is going to make it hard for anyone I know to recognize me. Of course, that was the idea. I would try to figure out a way to let my folks know I was ok, until the CIA did their job.

On the other side of the coin the DEA (drug enforcement agency) liked the idea of using surveillance aircraft to interdict drug operations, so they adopted it for their use.

Cherry-1 was shelved for now. Thinking to myself, I have to think up a new nick name. How about Cherry 2, or Cherry Wine, how about Cherry Blossoms, aha, Red Cherry. Yes, my new moniker was going to be "Red Cherry," it was kind of catchy don't you think? I think I'll name my new band "Clay and the Red Cherries." On second thought …maybe not.

I processed out of the military and along with my newly minted identity began acclimating back into civilian life. I had saved up quite a bit of money so I would be able to travel or whatever I wanted to do for a while.

I found a small town in the Midwest fairly close to home and settled in and began using the library to send out faxes still trying to find Cherry. With no luck. Of course, no one would know me by my new name here, so everyone should be safe for now. I anxiously awaited news from the CIA regarding the elimination of the Asian Drug Lord, who it turns out had operations in the US as well.

I missed 'Cotton Top' something terrible, I felt horrible that my family thought I was dead. I heard they had a memorial service scheduled.

I went home and was able to watch the service from a back seat in the crowded gymnasium at the High School. They said some really nice things about RJ. My poor mother was a wreck. I just hope this doesn't kill anybody till I can get my life back. I need to find a way to slip someone we both know, a note, telling them that I'm alive and well.

I had an idea, Bob and Larry are working at the feed store. I slipped in the back door and whistled a little tune I used to whistle while I worked there. It took a while, but Bob started searching for the sound. He was the most likely person to be able to keep a secret and share a secret at the same time.

I grabbed him by the shirt and dragged him into a back room. Startled he gasped for air when I covered his mouth. I shushed him and said, "Yeah, it's really me."

He squealed, "What the heck!"

I told him, "I'm being hunted by an East Asian Drug Lord and for the near future I'm playing dead. Here's my new name and current address, do not share that with anyone for the time being. I will give you a note to give to Tom, my brother. He's the most likely to be discrete."

The note said simply, "I'm alive and well. Do not attempt to contact me due to potential mortal danger for you and the family. I will get back to you when I can. Do not share this information with anyone unless it's a matter of life and death."

I left Bob with a huge grin on his face.

"Bob," I said. "Don't be too happy, this is not over yet. Bye"

I hovered close by as he called Tom on the phone asking him to come over to the feed store for a chat. They exchanged pleasantries, he gave Tom the note. Tom was taken aback but swiftly recovered quickly burning the note, and then left for home.

I dared not follow him or show my face around town any further.

Back to the fax machine. I think, I will try to put a little band together and tour around. Nothing else better to do. Firstly, I need to find a photo lab that will let me process my own film, being an amateur photographer and all, you know.

Secondly, I'm going to check with vehicle registration and see if the car, Cherry-1 has been re-registered. Turns out Cherry had not kept up with the registration. Which means it's probably under a tarp somewhere.

Thirdly, I'm going to find some property. Maybe a small farm, with a picket fence. Raise sugar beets or something. Get me a tractor, a barn, maybe a cow and name her Bessy.

Gentleman farmer Clay Ledbetter. Model citizen from the mid-west with money to burn and a life to live. What a grand idea, only I needed someone named 'Cherry' to kick start the conversation and share the joy. Please Lord Jesus, help us find each other again.

How does this name sound, "Clay Ledbetter and the Band Cherry" I don't know.

The band kicks off the mid-western stock car stadium tour next spring.

Chapter Fifteen

I landed in Australia for my next tour of duty. The hospitals in Australia are well run and almost identical in technology and methods as American hospitals. I found myself fitting in easily and took to the environment and conditions quite well.

"Welcome Captain Cherry Wilson to Australia and our grand hospital. Do you have a place to live and transportation." Quizzed the Hospital Administrator.

"Yes, I've found suitable accommodations and a small vehicle to get around in. The area is safe and the topography pleasant. I like the sea breeze coming in off the ocean in the morning and the beautiful sunsets. It helps keep me calm."

"If you don't mind me asking Miss Cherry, what do you do for entertainment on your off time?"

"I enjoy walks on the beach, listening to music, I do some water colors, mostly of the mountains of the east coast of America, my home."

"The work here is very hard and can be emotionally taxing at best and debilitating at worst. We rotate Doctors and Nurses out of here quite often due to emotional fatigue. Are you sure you're up to this type of work?"

"I worked with some burn victims in Vietnam before coming here. I don't think you can ever get used to it. It is however, a rewarding experience when they begin to recover. I've had my own tragedy of the heart and it actually helps me grieve and restore faith in God and myself. I will carry on and do my best.

My Airforce enlistment is up in eighteen months so I have that time to spend here and I intend to make the most of it. There are a good many American GIs, Airmen, Sailors, and Marines, under care in your hospital. I want to help as many of them as I can to get back home."

"It sounds like you are a good fit for our operations here. The reputation of your skills has preceded you; you indeed seem to have everything it takes to succeed here." Said the Administrator.

"My name is Colonel Marjorie Mills. If you have any need of assistance Captain Wilson, you have my number in your processing paperwork. Good day."

The sunsets are truly magical. They remind me fondly of the evenings I shared with RJ back home. Somehow, I knew in my heart he was still alive. My spirit was still yearning for his presence. I don't know why for sure it's, just how I feel. Absence any other information I will work and continue on until I see his name on a tombstone in the ground.

Work is good therapy for my soul. I have more than enough activities to stay busy and keep moving around.

I look into their eyes for any signs of life and hope. The ones that light up when I stop to see them, change their dressing, or take them to therapy are the ones most likely to recover and move on.

The ones that don't light up; I pray for their spirits and their bodies to mend. Many are beyond hope and that's awful for them and their families. However, there are plenty that want to get better; discussing thoughts of home, doing things like reading their mail to them, their home newspaper out loud, sends their spirits high.

One of the doctors invited me over to his apartment for a dinner. I paused for a second to gather my thoughts.

"What might your intentions be Doctor Smith?" I asked.

He replied. "I just thought you might need some company for a change. My intentions are only for a nice meal and some conversation about something other than work. I have a wife in the States, I don't need any of that type of companionship."

I replied. "I think I can fit something like that into my busy schedule. I must warn you I am an incurable romantic and there is a huge set of initials carved into the very bosom of my heart. RJ, Roy Jansen is my first, last and only lifelong love.

If I never see him again, or feel the gentleness of his touch, I will be a satisfied woman. That being said, I feel in my spirit that he's alive, my ongoing search, and a vault full of patience will eventually pay off."

He said, "Ground rules as they are. I will not harp endlessly on my sweetheart either."

"So how about dinner?" he asked.

"I can do that I suppose. I do warn you I'm not really as good a company as you might think. My heart and my head spin endlessly around the love of my life, 'RJ' and my quest to find him. Enough said."

Dinner went fine, it was a brief respite from the daily grind. There will be no more of that. I continue my work and try to bless the patients as best I can with my gentle touch.

As the patients are able to leave, many of them want to take me with them, sure that their mothers would just love me to death.

I just chuckle and send them on their way. The months passed quickly away. It was nearly time to go back to the states.

One day a few weeks before my stint here was up, I noticed some strange things going on. There are people following me, more than one sometimes. It seems as though they are almost following each other. Something is happening to my mail too.

I'd had enough. I went to the Hospital administrator's office and knocked on the door. She answered and invited me in. "What can I do for you Captain Wilson?" She asked.

"Are you having me followed?" I hissed between my teeth. "I've seen at least two men following me for the last three weeks. Believe me I've learned to spot them after my experience in Vietnam. Why are they following me?"

"Well Captain, what I'm about to tell you is highly confidential. I need you to sit down.

The only reason I'm divulging this to you is because you're about to leave. That boyfriend of yours RJ, Roy Jansen is alive. He is being hunted by an East Asian Drug Lord named 'Bac Thu'. RJ's 'FAC' team inadvertently targeted one of Bac's supply trains on the Ho Chi Min trail, it was subsequently destroyed, setting his operations back considerably. He found out who targeted him, he has sent agents to find and eliminate them in retaliation.

They tracked RJ and Lt. Gary Baker to Panama where they were serving out the rest of their enlistments, shot down their plane severely injuring the pilot, both RJ and Lt. Baker are weathered, but otherwise ok.

The CIA has taken over protecting them, which is one of the men following you. He is keeping an eye out for any of the Drug lords' agents. They would love to use you to find RJ and eliminate him. They would use any means possible to accomplish that.

RJ is now back stateside and has a new name and is forbidden to have contact with anyone who knows him for his safety and theirs. I cannot tell you any other information as it could endanger you. The CIA is working to find this elusive 'Bac Thu' and capture or kill him. He's apparently been quite a thorn in the side of many of the regional governments in SE Asia. We're not sure who the other man is, he could be one of Thu's agents.

Fighting back tears and gasping for breath. I have never been so happy and yet so stunned in all of my life. RJ, alive. He probably believes I think he's dead, and that I've stopped waiting for him, oh my God, this is crazy.

"Captain Wilson, you must remain calm and make no attempt to contact him or anyone of his family for the near future. Let the Agency do its job, you will soon be reunited."

Three more months and I rotate back to the states. I'm working to line up a burn victim hospital state side that could use my expertise.

I was beginning my packing when I got the strangest reply from one of my inquiries.

It read, "Captain Cherry Wilson, you are most cordially invited for an interview with our Human Resources staff when you return state side. Your outstanding reputation has preceded you. Our contact information is enclosed. By the way, someone else has been asking about you. We've received several faxes regarding your possible employment status here at our hospital. Hope to see you soon. Regards, Administrator Charles Wheelen."

Faxes...she wondered?

Chapter Sixteen

Tom went home after meeting with Bob and straight away collected Dad and spoke to him in a hushed tone. "Come with me." he said.

They loaded into the car and drove out into the country away from town.

"What the heck are you doing?"

Tom replied, "Dad, I have to talk to you, I had to make sure we weren't followed."

"Dad, RJ is alive and well. He's under CIA and FBI care, they've changed his name and told him to stay away from us for everyone's protection. There's an Asian Drug Lord after him, who could use anyone of us as leverage to get to him. They could be tapping our phones and getting into our mail. He had Bob at the feed store give me a note telling us a few details. What can you do?"

"Well Tom, I will have to reach out to some of my old contacts to get caught up on the situation."

"I knew you were CIA at some point in your life."

"Yeah well, it's actually how we ended up who we are, where we are, and with the Lazy J."

"Really!" Tom said. "Do you have a different name too?"

"Yes Tom, but that life is over and done with."

"Are the Grandparents even ours?" Tom questioned.

"Yes, they are, and the names we have are the names we live with."

"I will reach out to my old contacts to see if I can get a hold on the situation. This meeting never happened, right!"

"Yes Dad, it never happened. I am terribly excited for RJ. What about poor Cherry. She doesn't know he's alive and has grieved all this time. There has got to be a way to let her know the truth without spilling the beans to the Drug Lord."

"Give me some time son. I will find out what we can or cannot do. In the meantime, keep an eye out for people lurking about that don't seem to have any business here.

"Oh...well I've already seen a couple of characters hanging around asking questions. So far nobody knows anything, so we're safe. Except Bob, he could be an issue."

"How so?"

"He's beside himself with excitement, best news he's had in years, he said."

"We're going to have to get him a cover story, maybe his ship came in or something. We'll figure something out."

"Ok Tom, let's get on back before any one suspects anything."

As they drove back to town Dan explained his work in the early days after World War II and during the Korean war. He worked out of Long Beach harbor moving resources back and forth for the war effort in Korea. He worked as an inside man for the black-market trade smuggling anything that could raise money for the North Koreans, only he made sure it was tracked outside of the country. He helped smuggle some South Koreans out of the North and some assets back to the states.

"I retired after the Korean war was over and right before the Vietnam situation blew up into a full-scale war. I was hoping that war was going to be over before RJ or you would have to get involved. It's a miracle RJ has survived. It will be wonderful to get him back home.

Chapter Seventeen

"Rick Sheild, this is Dan., you might remember me as Sonny Bunch. I need a favor. Can I come and see you?"

"What's this about Dan?" asked Rick.

Rick is an agent of a government agency.

"Dan, meet me at the following address, make sure you're not followed."

"Got it," replied Dan.

Dan traveled to the location specified. He waited for the contact to show and use the prearranged passphrase.

He sat and waited for almost an hour when a shabbily clad man wandered up acting like he was drunk. He sat at the end of the bench and waited for another few minutes.

"Daisies are sure pretty this spring," the man said.

Dan replied, "Only when the sun shines from the west."

"My name is Larson, Rick Shield sent me, what's on your mind Dan?"

"You know good and well what's on my mind."

Larson sneered, "Oh ... the RJ thing."

"Yes, the RJ thing. He's my son and his mother and I are deeply concerned for his and Cherry Wilson's welfare, as well as our own. What have you got to say about that? I want to know the whole story, please start at the beginning, I'm a little slow these days."

"Okay Dan, this is what I can tell you."

"Don't mince words with me Larson, the whole story if you don't mind."

Larson clears his throat, "Senior Master Sergeant Roy Jansen and Lieutenant Gary Baker were on a routine mission off Laos. They inadvertently stumbled upon a supply train riding too close to the main trail. The supply train turned out to be one of Bac Thu's. He's a Drug lord, black market king pin, you name it. If it's illegal and makes money, he's in it up to his neck. The agency had been trying to track his movements for years. His home base could be anywhere from North Vietnam to Cambodia, Laos or Thailand. Evil and cruel doesn't describe this guy.

We've been trying to infiltrate his organization with little to show for it. And then, 'Cherry-1' nailed him, totally by accident. RJ and company never knew this of course, but what was done was done.

This got Bac all wound up, he started getting sloppy trying to figure out who targeted his supply train. He lost millions of dollars in cash and product because of it.

He has agents of his own everywhere. They managed to decode some voice traffic and discovered it was RJ and Gary that launched the attack.

He sent out agents to track them down. They didn't get close to them, but their unusual activity got our attention. We've been able to capture some of his guys and turn a couple of them to our side.

Captain Wilson, Cherry, was fed some false information to get her to stop looking for him. He didn't know this of course. He and Gary processed out of Asia to finish their enlistments in Panama.

Captain Wilson was devastated but she's a strong woman and bounced back ok. Her response of transferring to Australia actually worked in our favor. We monitored her and captured at least three of Bac's agents who were watching her, thinking she would lead them to RJ.

She was perfect bait, she thought RJ was dead so she didn't make any efforts to find him. RJ on the other hand didn't know where she was or how to get in touch with her so there are no loose ends there. Until."

"Until what?" Barked Dan.

Larson continued, "RJ was transferred to Howard AB in Panama to finish out his enlistment. He didn't know anyone was looking for him and Gary. He started sending out faxes to every hospital in the Northern Hemisphere trying to find Cherry.

One of his faxes got the attention of Bac's agents, they tracked him and Gary Baker to Howard AB. Before we could intercept them, they put together an op designed to take down some drug runners in the Panamanian jungle.

They had infiltrated the command infrastructure at Howard with a Commander Phillips and a Sergeant Lackey, along with a couple of Security Police. They dreamed up this night op getting close enough to RJ to get him to trust them enough to make it work.

RJ and Gary started to have some suspicions, but they didn't know Bac's people were tracking them, with a goal of eliminating them both in what was supposed to look like a training accident.

The three of them took off from Howard that night, they thought they were working a real op with a trainee.

The op was what you would consider normal until Sergeant Lackey painted the ground with a Laser. The next thing they knew an RPG (rocket propelled grenade) was up their tail pipe. The plane spiraled down into the jungle. RJ was bruised but otherwise unhurt, Gary had a collapsed lung, the Lackey fellow committed suicide.

They struggled through the jungle for weeks until they stumbled on a small village. They let them take refuge until Gary could heal up enough to continue traveling.

We tracked down the SPs, hoping we had all of them. We didn't know Phillips was the one in charge until RJ and Gary made it back to Fort Kobbe where they were arrested. Phillips tried to have them shot on sight, but our guys caught him first.

We had RJ and Gary go underground to make sure there were no more of Bac's agents around. Bac's guys thought RJ and Gary were dead so they dropped their guard. When Phillps found out they were still alive, we think he might have got off a garbled message to Bac's people.

Taking no chances, we gave them new identities, mustered them out of the service, and brought them back stateside. The FBI is now running the case. RJ's temporary name is Clay Ledbetter.

Captain Wilson turned out to be a great source of supply of foreign agents. She finally caught on and we had to read her in. She now knows that RJ is alive, but to protect everyone involved she doesn't know his new name ...yet.

Her enlistment was almost up so we arranged for her to transfer to the states. We're watching her closely to see if any of Bac's agents have found her. So far so good.

She is anxious to get back together with RJ...now that she knows he's alive. RJ has been explicitly told to stop faxing her. He's about out of his mind trying to find her, the boy is just going to have to wait.

In the meantime, we've got some guys inside Bac's organization. When the time is right, we intend to dismantle his organization bottom to top so that he will forget RJ and Gary ever existed. This Bac dude is bad news and carries one heck of a grudge. We're going to make it too expensive for him to continue the search. Even he has limits.

Cherry is processing out of the Airforce next week in California, she will be working in Utah at a Childrens hospital. Please don't try to contact her until this dirty business is over and everyone is safe.

RJ aka Clay, is living in Missouri, he's started up a little country pop band and is planning on touring around the mid and southwest playing gigs between car races at speedway events. He doesn't know anything about Cherry and it needs to stay that way for the time being. He only knows that she's alive and that she knows he's alive. That's all we can tell you for now. If you should stumble upon him stay away, Bac's agents may be tracking you. We've invested too much time, effort and resources to blow it now."

"Well Larson, that was a lot to take in. Is there anything I can do to help this along?"

"I'm afraid not. Just go home and live your life as if nothing different has happened and don't discuss this with anyone, because, the walls have ears. The FBI is handling the domestic side of this operation, from here on you will deal only with them. Good day Dan."

"Good day to you Larson, thanks for bringing me up to speed."

Dan drove the car home pondering what he might do next. One thing for sure he still had contacts and his own ways of dealing with things.

Thinking what his next move might be he sat down with Martha and discussed their options.

Martha said, in a hushed tone, the music playing loudly in the background, "This is dangerous Dan, for RJ, Cherry, and the rest of us. I don't want you meddling in this, but I know you, you'll have to do something."

"I'll think on it, Martha, I have experience in the import – export field of business from my old days with the Agency. I know some guys still active around Long Beach. I think I'll go out there and look em up, see what shakes out. Cherry is due to rotate back to Travis AFB any day now. If I know the Agency, they will try using her as bait to collect as many of Bac's operatives as they can."

Dan flew out to the coast dropping in on the local office of the FBI. He strode up to the front desk and asked to see the Agent in charge.

The worker at the desk asked him, "Do have an appointment sir?"

"No," Dan replied "you already know who I am and why I'm here, so let's get on with it, shall we."

Soon a well-dressed lady showed up and greeted him.

"Hello Dan, long time no see, wish you weren't here."

"Hello to you too, Elizabeth, can we take this elsewhere?"

"Sure, follow me," said Elizabeth.

"Woods, looks like you've done well. Agent in Charge now. That's something for sure."

"Well, she said, it's a target rich environment around here. You can hardly turn a corner without running into someone up to no good. It's made for some hard experience and fast advancement."

"The place could've used a woman's intuition all along," said Dan.

"What brings you here Dan?" Said Elizabeth.

"Oh, you surprise me Agent in Charge Woods, you know exactly why I'm here."

"Dan, you know I'm not supposed to discuss open cases with civilians."

"Well, this open case affects me and my family, if you think I'll sit back and do nothing, you've got another think coming."

"Ok, tell me what you know so far." Said Agent Woods.

Dan relayed what Larson had told him about the situation overseas.

"That matches up with what we know," said Agent Woods.

"So, what's the domestic take on this mess?" said Dan. "What have you got up your sleeve? This should be right up your alley. Catching bad guys with unsuspecting bait."

"Oh, come on now Dan, you know it was never like that."

"Spoken like a true operative, it never happened and this conversation never happened, blah, blah, blah."

"Ok you got me, what are we going to do on this one." Said Agent Woods. "The stakes are high all around. We want these bad guys locked up with enough proof to make it stick, get them off the streets, meanwhile you get your life back.

This Bac Thu guy has deep pockets and long reach, operatives everywhere, we've already bagged a few. They don't talk much, if they do flip, they can't be trusted. We have to take their identity and insert someone into the organization in a different location. The CIA is trying to do the same overseas. Bac knows we're on to him but he's determined to take RJ and Gary Baker down.

Fortunately, we've been able to get Baker and his family safely into protection. RJ is working with us too.

Captain Wilson is due in from Australia this week. We have a plan to collect her at the terminal, put her on another plane, and take her to the new location in Utah where she wants to work. Bac's people don't know that.

We're going to leak that she's incoming and put an operative in her place. Dressed up like her, white hair the whole bit. We're going to get the original Cherry-1 stingray out of storage at the Travis AFB impound lot, put it on a box truck under cover of darkness, truck it to your location, and put in storage. Hopefully there will be a joyful homecoming for the both of them in the near future.

We'll set her up with a secure place to live and a new car. She'll have twenty-four-hour surveillance and easy access to the most current information on her family, you guys, and RJ. She will still have to maintain covert silence until it's safe for everyone.

Our decoy will drive out of the gate at Travis driving a decoy red stingray and head to a setup in Arizona far away from the real deal.

We hope they take the bait, when they do ... they will mysteriously disappear. If we do our job and take out the domestic threat while CIA takes out the overseas threat, we can all go home, have an ice cream cone and a chocolate brownie.

We'll keep you informed on the status of the operation. We'll use dead drops and other means to communicate. What you need to do is track RJ's movements and make sure he's not breaking protocol.

Dan...we want this to succeed. Everyone needs to play their part. If any part of the plan goes sideways, we all lose.

Can you do that?" said Agent Woods.

"I can do that Elizabeth." Said Dan. "Giving me something to do is going to help keep me calm. I can handle that."

Dan traveled back home satisfied with what he's heard. He could do his part. Tracking Clay Ledbetter and the "Snake Skin Rangers" band, should be fairly easy.

Chapter Eighteen

Captain Wilson's (Cherry) plane landed at Travis AFB, taxied into a hanger with the doors shutting behind them. The planes door opened and she was met with a cadre of strangers wearing suits, except for one person who looked almost exactly like her, uniform and all.

"What's going on?" she asked.

"Hi, I'm Elizibeth Woods, Special Agent in Charge of the local FBI office. We're here to help you get back into civilian life as seamlessly as possible while eliminating the threat by Bac Thu's organization to you, RJ and your families.

Here's what's going to happen. Today you will go to a different hangar and board a plane for Utah and fly to the location of the hospital where you interviewed to work. When there you will get a new car and an apartment with twenty-four-hour surveillance.

Our decoy will assume your identity for the near future and drive a different red stingray out of the gate to Arizona where the decoy will assume working at a hospital there.

We hope she is followed by Bac's operatives. When they do, we will trail and capture them, interrogate them and put them in a dark hole. She will remain there for a few weeks until we feel that the threat has been neutralized.

You will go about your duties as if we're not there. Any questions?"

"Yes, when will I be able to see RJ?"

"Soon we hope," said Agent Woods. "If all plans are successful, you should be reunited within the year.

You will be able to follow his movements with information we provide you under coded messages. Let's go. We've got a lot of work to do."

The flight was routine, the landing unspectacular. She'd had time to think about the future and was eager to get to work in her new job. The apartment was nice and very comfortable. It was close to work so there was minimal travel time and less chance of exposure.

Cherry acclimated to her new surroundings and the work at the hospital. She set in for the long haul. She was extremely excited to see where RJ was on the map.

The decoy, Agent Emily Smith, zoomed out of the gate at Travis AFB, convertible top down, her hair blowing in the breeze. She stopped in the town of Fairfield just outside the gate where she found a hamburger joint and ice cream parlor. Making a rather big deal of her presence.

"Don't overdo it girl," crackled the voice in her earpiece.

"Yes ma'am," she barked back.

Agent Smith drove the alternate stingray down into the Oakland area and then caught the interstate to Arizona, stopping frequently along to way to see if she was attracting any attention. She attracted a lot of attention all right but not necessarily anyone whom the FBI was interested in. There was however a couple of chase cars that started to stand out.

"I'm pulling into a rest area for a few minutes, are you guys on those two chase cars?"

"Copy...Agent Smith, we've got them. If they do anything weird, we'll drop em."

"Ok I'm pulling over and parking, they've pulled in but are a way's back, about fifty yards I'd say. Wait, something is happening, one of them jumped out of his car and started motioning wildly towards me. He's found the pay phone and is making a call. What the devil is going on. Ok, they just screeched the tires and pulled a u turn out of the rest area. I'm getting out of the car to see what they're so excited about."

Agent Smith got out of the car and started walking around. She stopped and froze at the back of the car.

"Smith to Base, somebody forgot to switch out the license plate on the fake stingray. They know I'm not her. We're blown. On my way back to headquarters, Smith out."

The room exploded with a chorus of expletive words.

"What the heck happened, sneered Agent Woods."

The room got quiet.

"Nobody has an answer, nobody," Woods screamed.

"We're going to have to watch the real Cherry closer than ever now."

Our guys caught up with the two chase cars and followed them to their hideout. They set up a listening post and infrared to see what the situation was inside. We heard them jabbering to someone about the fake stingray. It was too hard to tell if it was someone inside or if they were on the radio or phone. We determined that their communications at this location was limited and there were about twenty well-armed occupants.

We waited until dark and movement inside was minimal. We made entry from several parts of the building with flash bangs and tear gas. They were caught off guard and we managed to capture them without any shots fired. Except the leader was able to drop down to a speed boat under the building and take off. The Coast Guard captured them a mile or so off shore.

Go and interrogate them please, and let me know immediately if you find out anything. It sounds like they might have got a message out to Bac's people before we collected them. We've got a lot more to worry about now.

Cherry has been getting updates on RJ's movements. If they snatch her this whole thing could go sideways. Bac's people think the Airmen are dead, at least they weren't sure whether they are or not. If they get her the whole thing blows up. We have to shore this up...now.

Woods banged her fists on the desk, "After all the planning how could we let his happen? Whose job was it to get that done anyway?"

A rookie agent stepped up and claimed responsibility.

"Actually ma'am, somebody took off with the car while I was getting ready to change the plate."

"Why the heck didn't you say anything?"

"I didn't think it was that big of a deal, I mean really." Said the rookie.

"Details are critical rookie; they can make or break even the simplest of ops," Woods spewed angrily.

"Now we have to make a new plan. Get Dan, RJ's dad on the phone. We need to read him in."

"Dan this is Woods."

"Hello Woods, what have you got for me? I hope its good news for once."

"It is good news. We tried the decoy op; it worked out a bit differently than we expected. Bac's guys identified our decoy and sped off; we tracked them to their office in a warehouse in the dock district at Long Beach harbor. We made entry and captured them, including all of their intel, communications devices, product and weapons. Carted it all away for analysis. It was a treasure trove.

"That is good news Woods. Where do we go from here?"

"We're going to double the guards on Cherry and monitor her closely until we're sure the domestic threat is over."

"Whoa don't do that. I have a different idea. There's a small gathering scheduled to memorialize the FAC guys from the Vietnam conflict over at Wright Patterson AB in Ohio in a few days.

Let her out to attend that, we can watch from there. She needs some contact with our people and a few hugs would help too. She needs to know we are all still in this together. We might even be able to arrange for her parents to join us.

I'll send you the details, you can arrange for her to just show up at the event. If none of Bac's people show, we can safely say it's done. The CIA still has a lot of work to do. It appears from my last conversation with Larson that Bac's organization has closed ranks and is ghosting their suppliers. Probably because of what you accomplished on the west coast.

Bring her to the event, we can manage security from there. Too many people looking like FBI agents would likely spook them anyway. Since it's a military sponsored event, a lot of people dressed in uniform wouldn't be noticed."

"I don't know Dan; it seems pretty risky."

"The world is constantly changing Woods, the only thing that makes it worth living is for us to take bold action to mold it. If we keep waiting for Bac to make a move we will be frozen in time. We just can't abide that any longer.

Talk to her, if she doesn't want to come, we'll understand."

"Ok, I understand. I will go see her, if she's ok with it, I will make the arrangements. Good bye Dan."

"Let me know as soon as you can, I will get with the admin at 'Wright Pat' to set it up. Best wishes Woods."

Chapter Nineteen

"Miss Wilson, this is Agent Woods from the FBI. We need to have a chat. Can I come see you tomorrow?

"Yes...that would be fine," said Cherry. "What's this about?"

"I'll tell you when I see you tomorrow, we can't discuss it over the phone. See you tomorrow."

Cherry's thoughts are racing, it had been so long since there was any news.

She could hardly wait till tomorrow.

"Hello Miss Wilson, I'm Agent Woods and this is Special Agents Renfroe and Smith, they will be staying in the apartment next to yours. They are going to be your contact from here on. Agent Smith is going to be your double on certain occasions.

We believe the domestic threat against RJ and you of course, are finally over. We're going to remain vigilant for the near future but, we are going to let some air in on the issue.

Two weeks from now there is a gathering scheduled at Wright Patterson AFB in Ohio to honor Veterans of FAC activity in Vietnam. If you would like to go to the event, we can arrange for you to attend."

"Try and stop me," said Cherry. "You can call me Cherry please."

"Since you put it that way, here's the details that we know for now."

Agent Woods detailed the plan that Dan had presented to her.

"What do you think Cherry?" said Woods.

"I will need a new wardrobe; can you arrange a shopping trip? I've not seen the inside of a store in years."

"Yes, I believe we can make that happen; Agent Renfroe will see to all the details. Happy shopping ladies. I will debrief you when you return from Ohio. Good bye for now."

Cherry and Agent Renfroe climbed into the Limousine, while Agent Smith went to a different mall on the opposite side of town. The Limo drove them to the nearest shopping mall.

"This is so fun," giggled Cherry. "Don't you think so Agent Renfroe?"

"Please call me Marsha, yes it's fun, but it's also work for me so don't get too wild and crazy girl."

Agent Renfroe had been in the Agency for over ten years. She was broad shouldered in the sense that she could handle a variety of responsibilities with confidence. She was a skilled marksman and hand to hand combat.

She and Cherry hit it off pretty quick, mostly due to her emotional and intellectual maturity. She sensed Cherry's attitudes and emotions pretty quickly making the tasks that much easier.

"Marsha," quizzed Cherry, "How did you wind up in the FBI?"

"I suppose I would say its generational. My Father and Mother were both in the service in one form or another. My brother is an Agent with the NSA doing whatever they do. Top Secret stuff. I haven't really thought about doing anything else. I like helping people and protection of individuals like yourself is what I love doing. At the end of the day if it's just another normal day then I've done my job.

My family moved around the country frequently so I'm not attached to anyone part of it. I do like Colorado though and if we get a chance, I'd like to take you skiing. Would you like that?"

"Sure," said Cherry, "I used to ski on the east coast around New York on weekends when I was younger. That would be fun."

The driver let them out at the front of the mall. "I'll be parked over there under that tree on the other side of the parking lot, just give me a call on the radio when you're ready to go."

They got out of the limo and entered the first store. A department store full of everything you could ever have dreamed of.

Cherry stopped in her tracks, her eyes full of wonder, her next steps was cheerful and happy. She was absolutely floating on air.

"Oh, Marsha," squealed Cherry. "This is incredible. The smells and all the colors, it's just grand. I might even get a swimming suit."

Marsha, agent Renfroe, just smiled and flashed the plastic credit card they would use today to get her everything her heart desired, within reason of course.

"I've worn nothing but uniforms for years," said Cherry, "this will be quite a treat. Oh, my they even have pretty dresses. I must try some of them on.

After making several selections, and browsing every department in the store. They had armloads of shoes, hats, pants, jeans, tops, and some beautiful dresses. After taking a pause Marsha suggested they go to the food court in the center of the mall for some lunch.

"Food court," exclaimed Cherry, "they have food here too."

They ordered some sub sandwiches and chips and soda, sat down and ate their food. The food court was busy with people coming and going, laughing and chatting with one another. Things Cherry had not experienced in a very long time. She was aglow with amazement.

Agent Renfroe's head was on a swivel, she was starting to get weary. However, Cherry's energy was propelling them onward. They visited stores with furnishings, and all sorts of nick knacks for a household.

"Before we go, I just need one more thing," said Cherry. "I want some of RJ's favorite perfume. Heavenly Scented, do you know where we can get some?"

"It's a fairly popular scent Cherry, I believe it's sold in the first department store we came into. On our way out we can stop and make that your last purchase."

"Oh, that would be wonderful. I've had such a great time Marsha. I'm going to go back and try everything on and start packing."

Agent Renfroe called for the driver who met them at the door. She suspiciously surveyed the area. The driver answered, "Copy."

The driver pulled up to the store front.

"Who are you," yelled agent Renfroe, snatching her concealed weapon from its location behind her back, pointing it at his head as she shoved Cherry back out of the way.

"Whoa there, cowgirl," said the Driver. "I'm the relief driver. You were in there so long I had to relieve the other driver."

"Why wasn't I told about this?" Renfroe said.

"You were briefed at the meeting earlier, weren't you paying attention?"

"Well, somebody should have let me know when it happened."

"Radio silence, Renfroe, remember."

"Ok, no threats, let's go," she told the driver.

Everyone was still on edge around Cherry's apartment and workplace. Bac's people had a tendency to pop up out of nowhere and steal the day right out from under you.

"Not this day," said Cherry. "This day was wonderful, thank you so much Agent Renfroe for such a magical time."

Later that week Cherry and Agent Renfroe traveled by airline to Ohio where the event was to occur. There she met Dan and Martha and her parents Deb and Joe Wilson from Cape Cod.

"Oh my God Cherry," gushed her mother, "when is this cloak and dagger business going to be over?"

"It's almost done mom," said Cherry, "almost done. Let's enjoy our time together as it is. Everyone is working hard to put an end to the nightmare. This is Agent Renfroe, she's my escort for the near future."

"Pleased to meet you, Agent. I trust you are protecting our baby closely? How did we get into this mess anyway?" quizzed Deb.

"Yes, ma'am I am. I'm afraid it is a very long story; one that Cherry can share with you some other time. We hope this whole affair is over soon."

Cherry ran over and hugged Dan and Martha, Lanora had her little ones with her and her husband. Tom came up as well, all smart looking in his airline uniform.

"How are you, Cherry?" said Tom.

"I'm fine," said Cherry, "I'm just a bit anxious for this affair to be over. This event is a much-needed change of pace, I really needed this. I sure wish RJ was here."

"Pretty soon Cherry," said Dan. "He's got a little band of Vets together and they're touring the country working through some old trauma. Their music is helping them all heal. He'll be back with us soon."

The event was somber and crisp. FAC operatives' names were read and saluted, a twenty-one-gun salute was sounded. RJ and 1st Lt. Baker's names were read as Missing in Action.

Tears flowed abundantly for them and all their comrades in arms. The event ended with a trumpeter playing taps. They all retired quietly from the area.

Dan met briefly with the Base Commander and exchanged greetings. Dan caught him up on what was going on with Bac's organization and the efforts to end the horrible situation permanently. As he turned to leave a uniformed man motioned over to him.

"Hi, my name is Sergeant Ballard. I flew with Roy in the early days when he first arrived in-country. He was a bright eyed and naïve youngster full of himself and eager to get the job done. I enjoyed working with him and am sad to hear about all he's been through. I was able to meet with Cherry for a few minutes when she was in Da Nang. I'm glad to see she's doing well. I'll be off now. Best of luck to you all."

The families met for dinner that night at the hotel where they're staying.

Cherry went up to her room to freshen up. When all of a sudden, some guy jumped her and tried to drag her away.

"Oh no you're not buster," she screamed, as she hauled off and knocked the guy right off his feet and started kicking and punching him.

He started yelling for someone to get her off him. One of the hotel security police dragged him off. Local police had him jailed before you could say 'handcuffs.'

Agent Renfroe came running up all out of breath and blurted out, "Someone just tried to snatch Cherry. Thankfully...Cherry stopped him, knocked the guys block off, that's one tough chick. Turned out to be some random dude trying to abduct young women."

"Oh my God," sighed Martha, "what's the world coming too? Is she ok?"

"She's fine, she's getting dressed now, one of the other agents is guarding the room. She'll be along shortly."

"I think I'm going to have a nervous breakdown before this is over," muttered Deb.

Joe asked Dan, "How have you handled all this so far? It's about to make us nuts."

Dan answered him, "When you love someone dearly, you don't mind the weather, rain or shine."

The next day they all said their goodbye's and headed for home, in Cherry's case, back to work at the hospital in Utah.

"Before you go Cherry, I want you to know how much we love you," said Martha.

Dan gave her a hug and told her, "RJ is ok and will be off this phase of his journey soon. He misses you terribly. As soon as we get the all clear from the CIA, he's coming home."

Her tears flowing again, she sobbed quietly. "I miss him so much Dan."

"I know sweetheart, we all do, safe travels Cherry, we'll see you soon." Said Dan.

She walked down the boarding ramp for her flight, looking back one more time to wave goodbye.

Chapter Twenty

RJ...I mean...Clay set up his apartment in a small city in Missouri named Springfield. Nice town it seemed. Mostly it was not too far from home, if he got the yearning.

The FBI has reduced its presence as of late. Something must have happened on the home front to eliminate that threat. Hopefully it was good for everyone else, especially Cherry.

Anyway, I'm going to explore the local area, and search for a used bus to tour around in with my, as yet unnamed music group. There are some good restaurants in town and lots of sporting activities, boating, fishing, hunting, in the area.

My hope was to find a few guys willing to play some down-home American music and tour around for a while. I still needed to give the CIA time to shake off the Drug goons in Asia. Can't hardly wait for that. In the meantime, I heard there's a small-town south of Springfield called Branson. I'm hoping I can go there and get some pointers from some of the musicians there on how to run a tour group.

First, I need to go get those pictures of home, my Cherry car and my Cherry girl developed and plastered on my walls. Those pictures make good wall paper. I also have a small photo I put on the neck of my guitar so I can always be reminded of what I'm living for.

The FBI hooked me up with a pickup truck so I would blend in with the locals. It was an old Ford truck. It wasn't much to look at but it had a nice V8 engine with a four-barrel carburetor. It could get me out of trouble if the need arises.

I got up and made some breakfast and then got ready and drove over to the grocery and picked up some supplies and a phone book. Cruised around town for a few hours taking in the sights. Went back to the apartment and made some lunch. Afterwards I got on the phone nosing around for the nearest Veterans Center. Those guys had local contacts and might even be able to connect me with some talent that's interested in making some music and taking in the scenery.

That afternoon I went over to the Vet center and walked in.

"Hey," I said, to the young lady manning the front desk.

She said, "Hey," back.

This was going to be an interesting conversation I thought.

"What can I do you for," she muttered.

"Hi my name is Clay. I'm new here around these parts, I thought I would come down here and see what's shakin."

I read her name tag; it said Terry, so I called her by her name.

She jumped back and scolded me, "How do you know my name?"

"Uh...it's on your name tag," I said timidly.

"Oh sorry," she said, "I forget about that thing."

"Well Clay, not much is shakin today. Most of the guys are day workers or they are over at the hospital in Joplin getting treatment. It's usually pretty quiet around here during the day.

There's some pool tables and stuff around the corner in the day room if you want to hang out. There's coffee and pastries also if you're hungry.

"Thanks Terry," I said. "I'll check it out, go get my feet wet...if you know what I mean."

"Knock yourself out," she replied.

I went around the corner and just like she described there were tables for games and refreshments. I really wasn't there for games or food; I could use a cup of coffee though. What I was really there for was to find a brain or two to pick for information.

There are a few guys scattered around the large room; reading magazines or drinking coffee or chatting with each other.

I picked up a pool cue. I didn't really want to play but I figured if I fooled around with it someone might approach me for a game. I could then strike up a conversation. Best not to be too pushy. No one knew me and trust was a really big issue with some of these guys.

I knocked the balls around on the table, pretending to be really focused on my game. I managed to make more noise than friends. I dropped the cue and went back over and poured myself another cup of coffee, it was actually surprisingly good.

I felt the presence of someone behind me. My spine tingled for an instant. I abruptly turned around.

"Whoa, there fella, I just need some of that, there coffee myself."

I moved out of his way and went and found a seat. He followed me and sat down a few feet away.

"What's yer name stranger," he asked.

"Clay," I replied.

I thought o...k...another scintillating conversation to follow.

"I'm Roger, I kind of see to things around here. Make sure nothing hinky is going on. We don't drink alcohol or do drugs here. Except on the third Saturday of each month when beer is allowed, we have a little dance for the locals. We try to get the vets and the locals to mix and mingle a bit.

I'm a Korean war veteran, there are a few WWII vets around, most of the younger guys are Vietnam vets."

"What's your story Clay?" Asked Roger.

I had to think quick, hadn't thought about having to come up with a story. Had to be careful not to make up anything too hard to remember. I figured Roger could sniff out a lie in a heartbeat. I paused for a second, hung my head, and told him.

"I spent some time in Vietnam, Thailand and around, doing some Airforce stuff. Aircraft maintenance mostly. Nothing too dangerous. I was an Avionics Maintenance Specialist – Airborne Navigational Aids repairman. Serving in the Tactical Air Command."

Other Airforce vets always want to know where you were stationed and what aircraft types you worked on. It was almost like a lie detector test.

"So, what aircraft types did you work on Clay?" Quizzed Roger.

"Well, I said, let's go down the list. A-1's, A-26's, C-119, C-123 and C-130 gunships and transports, O-1's, O-2's, OV-10's. There were a few others but that was mostly what I worked around."

"When were you there?" Roger continued the test.

"'71' through the beginning of '73.'"

"Sounds like you did some time around Da Nang, Cam Ranh, and NKP."

"Yea...that about covers it."

"I think there's some of the guys around here that were in and around those locations as well, you might know a couple of them. They were there about the same time. I'll introduce you later if you want.'

"Sure," I said, "be interesting to connect with somebody from the zone."

Oh yikes, I thought. Never dawned on me I might run into anybody from over there at the same time. This could get dicey.

"When do the guys show up around here. I'd like to meet some of them and catch up. I would love to see if any of them are into music. I'm putting together a small music group to play and tour around for a while. Kinda...want to get back into the swing of things and see the country."

"Talking is good for most of them and they would enjoy your company. Some are pretty shaken up still and have a pretty light trigger. We just try to make them comfortable and get them headed toward the best treatment for their situation. You'll be able to spot them fairly quick. Others are working with some physical injuries from amputations to hearing and sight.

If you came back around six o'clock this evening you can see for yourself.

"I'll be upfront with you Roger; music saved my life when I got out of the zone. My nerves were shot, I could barely put two thoughts together. I stumbled onto an old guitar at the hospital during my recovery and started strumming the thing. The vibration and tone from the strings really calmed my brain. Even put some songs together after a while."

"Sounds interesting Clay, I'm sure the guys would be glad to hear you play. You can play...right?" He asked tentatively.

"Oh yeah, I'm no Dusty Redfield or anything but I can carry a tune.

"So, what' your story Roger?" I asked.

"Humm, well I served with the 1st Marine Division at the battle of Chosin Reservoir. The weather was horrible and the Chinese tried to wipe us out. We managed to turn and fight our way out to the coast where there were ships waiting for us. We lost most of the Division and nearly all our equipment. I lost a couple of toes to frost bite. It was not a glorious battle by any means. I'm thankful to have survived."

I was a bit stunned listening to him talk about his story. I am beginning to understand why many of them don't like to talk about their war time experiences. What do you say to someone who's been to hell and back? Thank you for your service seems a little bit weak. But it's better than sitting there with your jaw on the floor. In retrospect a simple thank you may be the best any one individual can say to show gratitude for service to our fellow man.

"Truly Roger, thank you for your part in the service of our country."

"I'll see you this evening, I'll even bring my trusty instrument along. See you then."

I really need Roger to trust me. If I can break the ice with him, I can hopefully open a new chapter in this journey to sanity. Gonna go see if I can check out a used bus, I saw advertised in the paper this morning.

I drove around for a while and finally found the address of the person with the used bus. I knocked on the door and introduced myself. We went over to a used car lot where I checked out the bus, and walked away pretty quickly. Not what I was hoping for. The guy did say he knew of one close by that sounded more the style I was looking for. I found that address and knocked on the door.

Seemed like I waited forever when this elderly gentleman finally answered the door.

"Hey there mister, what can I do for ya,"

"I got your name from Willy in town, he said you might have a bus I was looking to buy. Any truth to that?" I replied.

"Well, she's in back next to the barn, I used her to do some cross-country touring of my own. The wife and I would take off every spring and go somewhere we'd never been before. She died last winter of the flu. The bus has been sitting quietly next to the barn ever since. It's just not the same touring without her.

You might have to run some squirrels out of the engine compartment, and you really need to pay attention to the wiring.

"My name is Clay; I'm staying over in Springfield for the time being, I want to put together a little music group. The bus needs to sleep four or five and be able to carry instruments and luggage."

"Earl's my name; let's go take a look at her. She's just around here."

We made our way to the back of the lot next to a big red barn, and sure enough the bus was there. My eyes started to sparkle with anticipation. I walked around it and surveyed the outside, the tires looked in good shape, the windows are all ok. I popped the door to the engine compartment in the back of the bus. It was a diesel engine, looked pretty clean actually.

Sure enough, we scared off a nest of squirrels. I checked out the wiring pretty thoroughly, not finding anything scary. A couple of hoses could use a refresh.

I asked Earl, "Is there enough fuel in her to start her up?"

He replied, "I think so, it was pretty full when I parked her. I'll go grab the keys."

While Earl was looking after the keys, I opened the door and looked inside. They had put in a galley kitchen with room for a small fridge. One of those new cookers, a microwave they call them could help make hot food.

There was already space for four beds. Five if I made some adjustments. This will do, I think. Now then...will she start?

Earl moseyed back with the keys.

"Start her up, there Clay."

I cranked the engine and pumped the gas pedal a couple of times. It sputtered and coughed reluctantly.

"Might be a little moisture in the fuel," Earl said. "Try er again."

I pumped the gas pedal a couple more times and turned the key, it cranked this time. A cloud of blue smoke belched out the back end. After a brief warm up it purred like a kitten.

"The only thing left to do here Earl is discuss how much it was going to take to let me ride around the country in er for a couple of years."

"Make me an offer," he said.

"How about $1000 even?"

He smarted back, "how about $1100 and you can ride out of here right now."

I popped back, "How about $1050?"

"Oh, all right, that sounds pretty fair."

We went back in the house and did the paperwork, afterward I drove back to town. I would get someone from the apartment complex to drive me over and pick the bus up tomorrow.

It was almost six o'clock, I wanted to go the Vet Center and meet some guys and maybe play a couple of songs with em.

I pulled up outside in my pickup truck, I parked it alongside what seemed like a hundred other pickup trucks. Grabbed my guitar case and went inside.

Terry the receptionist was there giving out name tags and steering people to the food buffet.

"Hello again," I told her.

"Oh...I wasn't sure you'd come back. Lots of guys come, when they find out we don't do alcohol, they move on."

"Look, I'm more than ok with that. I like to keep a clear head. Give me a good cup of coffee and I'll be fine."

I had a lot of reasons to avoid alcohol. The FBI guy parked across the street was not too keen on it. I needed my wits about me, just in case of a rumble, and I think I might even be allergic to it. If the social occasion required it, I would either bow out, or carry around a glass in my hand and pretend to sip it.

"So, what's on the buffet tonight, Terry," I asked.

"Oh…it's the Wednesday night usual, brisket, beans, and potato salad."

"Yummy, sounds good."

I went around the corner and got some food and a drink of ice tea. Went over and sat down and made myself comfortable at a long dining table.

About half way through the meal a guy down the row from me opened a conversation.

"Hey there sailor, where ya from," he said.

Not wanting to divulge too much information I smarted off.

"I'm from the east side of town."

"Well slick, that's not exactly what I meant, but have it your way."

At seven o'clock a few guys gathered in a corner with some instruments, a drum set, couple of guitars, a fiddle and a banjo. They played a few songs while people listened and continued their meals.

After an hour or so one of them said, "We're going to take a quick break. When we get back maybe ole Clay over here will join us for a set."

I tuned up the twelve string and got up on the little stage with the guys, we introduced ourselves and struck up a familiar tune.

We played several cover songs until the crowd started to dwindle.

I was breaking my strap down when one of the fella's came up and introduced himself as Curt.

I said, "Hey Curt, how's it going? Was I any good tonight?" I asked.

"Pretty good I'd say, I enjoyed it."

"Did you have something else on your mind?"

That was about the time I noticed the burn scar on his arm.

"Uh...yeah, I noticed that snap shot on the neck of your guitar. Who is that, he queried."

"Um...she's a good friend of mine from back home."

"That picture and the plate on the car, Cherry-1 seems awfully familiar."

"How so?" I asked.

"Well, I think you noticed the scar on my arm. When I was in hospital in Australia there was a nurse that looked exactly like her. I believe her name was Cherry Wilson, she was a Captain. Like many others I tried to court that girl before I left. Like all the others she made it clear she was sweet on one guy. A forward air controller, call sign Cherry-1. Is that the same girl?

"Well, that would be an incredible coincidence, wouldn't it Curt."

"I'll tell you what man, that girl walks on water around here. She helped quite a few of the guys get well and get home whole.

That fella of hers, the FAC guy call sign Cherry-1, is a legend. He saved the lives of many a downed aircrew. I heard though, that he ran into a spot of trouble, he and his pilot buddy. They tangled with a regional drug lord or something like that and stirred up quiet a hornet's nest. You wouldn't happen to be that guy, would you?"

Curt stared at me for a minute expecting an answer.

"I don't know what to tell you man. The picture is a friend of mine from back home. The car was one of my buddies from school. I just really liked the picture. Kind of reminds me of what I want out of life.

He retreated with a very suspicious look in his eye.

"Well if you ever run into that guy or the girl in the picture. Let them know we would love to have them over for dinner and maybe even a parade."

"Trust me Curt, if that should ever happen, I will let them know."

The FBI guy crackled in my earpiece, "Good dodge man. We're out of here. No more Vet Centers for a while ok."

"Copy that."

I said my goodbyes at the center, hopped in my truck and sped away. Someday I might take Curt and the guys up on that invitation.

Next day I had someone from the apartment complex where I as staying help me go get the bus. I waved to Earl as I smoked the tires on my way out of the drive. Well...that might have been the engine smoking, no matter, off we go. I had a lot of work to do.

I parked the giant jelly bean across the street from the apartment. From a distance it looked like a giant jelly bean. The "Bean" needed a bath, a new paint job, some interior work and then it would be ready to hit the road.

I hand stenciled the band name on the side of the bus. Clay Carter and the Snake Skin Rangers. I choose the stage name Clay Carter because it was shorter and the band name Snake Skin Rangers because it just sounded cool. Clay Ledbetter would still be my mailing address for the near term. I say term because the situation with the CIA and their target needs to wrap up, like a short term of time. Like a semester term. Get it done guys.

After a couple of weeks of special attention, the "Bean" was ready to go. I drove her down to the truck stop to fill up with fuel.

I was standing there counting the dings on the pump when this guy shows up out of nowhere, leans against the bus and speaks.

"I know who you are man. I know you."

I looked over at him and said, "Is that so."

"Who might I be?"

"You're that rock star that disappeared a couple years ago. They say he went underground to escape attention."

"Is that so," I said. "Well how much would it take for you to keep my secret. Fifty, a hundred?"

"Awe heck man, I don't want your money."

"What do you want then?"

"I want a job man. I want to drive your bus around, be your agent. Help you find gigs and stuff man."

"Can you work on a diesel engine if needed?" I asked him. "How about loading stuff in and out?

"Sure, I can do all that."

"So let me get this straight. You want a job in exchange for keeping my secret. You will load out and drive the bus and do the agent thing for gigs?

"You got it man."

"Is there anything else you want besides all that?"

"I'd still like that fifty, I could use some new tennis shoes."

"What am I to call you?"

"Bud...Bud will do."

"You're right Bud, I am a rock star from the past and I'm defiantly ducking attention from unwanted sources. However, I'm ready to come out of hiding and assume a new identity and make some music and have some fun. Are you up for all that?"

"You got it man," said the newly minted friendship...Bud.

"Ok Bud, call me Clay. I'm going to finish gassing up the bus, I'll meet you over there on the other side of the parking lot."

Bud trotted off to get himself some new tennis shoes. Wait...fifty bucks for tennis shoes.

I finished the fueling and checked the tires and other fluids. I came around the front and stepped up in the front door and jumped back.

"Well now. Who might you be," I mused, as I looked at the charming little face of what appeared to be a Jack Russel dog...sitting in my drivers' chair. He looked to be about two or three years old and well fed. I checked for a collar. Nope, no collar.

I tried to coax him down and out. No such luck. I was about to give up when Bud arrived and chuckled, "I see you've met Piper."

"Ahh, yes, I guess I have."

"Come here Piper, here boy," called Bud.

Piper hopped down and took a seat behind Bud.

"Ok, well we've got another mouth to feed. Did you account for him on your grocery list, there Bud?"

"Oh yea, he was coming all along, I just forgot to tell you. I hope that's ok."

This day is getting weirder by the minute.

"Ok Bud, make yourself useful and drive us down to Branson."

"Yes sir," When he smiled, his face sparkled like an explosion of confetti. That was weird, if I didn't know better, I might think Bud was an Angel or something.

Bud was a tall lanky fellow with dark brown hair and blue eyes. He was well nourished and muscular; from my first impressions he seems to be incredibly intelligent and confident. Something about him, a feeling mostly. Like I already knew him from somewhere.

The drive to Branson was fairly short but the two-lane road and the seriously steep hills were quite a test of the Bean's abilities. We made it safely into town and cruised around for a time looking for an empty theater we could use to audition some potential band mates and then practice for a few days.

We found one that was empty and had a sign out front. I called the agent and asked if we could rent the venue for about ten days. They agreed, we signed a paper and set up shop.

It wasn't a big theater but it was just right for our needs. Bud parked the bus out front where it could be easily seen from the street. He then started searching the trade magazines for anyone looking for a short-term stint with a traveling band.

Just when I thought I couldn't get any more surprised Bud pops back in and says he needs the keys to the pickup truck. In another grand piece of luck, the bus came with a tow bar for the pickup.

After a few hours, it was getting dark outside and I hadn't seen Bud for a while. He came roaring up with a big smile on his face. I stood there waiting for the explosion of confetti. He just chuckled.

"I hope you got us something to eat in your many travels?" I spoke. "Piper was looking longingly at my leg and licking his chops."

"Oh, way better than that," blurted Bud. "Here's some pizza, you know the kind you like. And I found some guys interested in what we want to do. They'll be around tomorrow to check you out and discuss particulars."

"Awesome," I said. I thought how does he know what kind of pizza I like?

The next morning, I had to check in with my FBI contact. "Say," I asked, "are you getting all this." He just laughed.

"Who do you think suggested to him what kind of pizza you like."

"Thank God, I thought I was losing it. Have you already run background checks on the band prospects?"

"Sure have, you're clear. Of course, they might not like you." He snickered.

Three guys came dragging in about ten o'clock am. I greeted them with a smile and a handshake.

"Hey guys, I guess Bud told you what we're hoping to do. Are you all ok with that?

They all shook their heads in agreement.

"Well let's get to know one another shall we."

There was Ed on bass guitar, Nick on drums, and Zane on lead guitar.

Ed was from the east coast, somewhere around the New York area. He could play a mean bass. A very bright guy with a heavy New York accent and a prankish sense of humor. Nick on the other hand seemed kind of quiet, he was sort of a local from the Kansas City area. If you needed a beat, he had one ready to go, sometimes he could be a nuisance banging on everything. A real drummer's drummer.

Zane, on lead guitar, had long hair and said 'Dude' a lot. They all seemed to already know each other, like they had been playing together somewhere before. Zane's approach to playing the lead was harmonic and melodic as well as very musical. I found out pretty quick I could just sit and listen to him play for hours.

I also discovered that Bud literally had the voice of an angel. He was going to sing lead as well as all his other duties.

I was clearly the amateur in the group.

"Gather around guys, I'm going to play rhythm and sing backup. Let's tune up and play something simple to get started."

"One, two, three."

Out came the most awful screech you've ever heard in your life.

"I have an idea. I'm going to play a series of tones, just relax and let the sound just fill your soul."

I played some of the tones I'd heard when I was in hospital working to rehab.

After ten minutes or so they all looked a little more at ease.

"Ok let's try it again."

So far so good. The music started to blend and before I knew it the sound was downright harmonic. We practiced for the next few days, on the end day, I looked up and to my surprise, the theater was half full of people. Oh wow, that just made the day that much sweeter.

After we finished our set, we made some introductions and thanked everyone for coming out. Probably Bud's doin.

The next day I called the guys together.

"Here's what we plan to do. I've already spelled out how you will get paid. We will send money orders back to a local bank and keep enough cash on hand to operate. When we're done, we will cash out and split the take, everyone ok with that? Good...over the next couple of days we will map out a series of stops at local venues such as county fairs and stock car race tracks. When the weather starts getting cold, we will move further south. I plan to run this show for a calendar year from now. After that I will drop you back here and we split up. Sounds good?"

They all signaled their agreement.

First of all, we need to hit Kansas City for some Snake Skin Cowboy Boots, and maybe a hat if they've got em.

They all crowed, "Yee haw."

Oh...this ought to be fun.

I snuck out and met with the FBI guy. "Man...have you heard anything from the Asian op?"

"Sorry," he said. "I know they are getting staged for a major operation as soon as the rainy season is over. Couple a months' maybe. Hang on man. It won't be much longer."

We plowed down the interstate towards Kansas City, pulled into the parking lot of a big western store, piled out, went in and got fitted for some new duds.

While there, the owner asked us who we were.

Bud declared, "We're the Snake Skin Rangers and we're ready to rock the town."

Next thing we know we're in the parking lot of a huge barbecue restaurant jamming with the locals. I confess it was a lot of fun.

So it went, town after town, we played before the stock car races at small towns and hit some county fairs across Iowa and Nebraska. The band actually had no idea I was searching for any sign of Cherry the car, or Cherry the girl.

It was starting to cool down so we drifted down to Oklahoma and New Mexico, ended up in Texas for a couple of months till the worst of the winter weather was over.

We stopped at a small town in south Texas to play a gig at a decent sized Race Track. Bud pulled the bus into the empty parking lot. It was the day before the races so it was quiet. We had some business to do with the owner before the event.

The owner came out to meet us after we parked. He showed Bud where to put our stuff.

"I need to speak to the leader...Clay, is it?"

I got down out of the bus and introduced myself as Clay. I instantly recognized the owner. I motioned him quickly to where he needed me to sign papers for the contract of the gig.

"Hey there Sergeant Ballard, how ya doin?"

He stuttered and stammered for a few seconds. "RJ...is that you?"

"Yeah, it's me. I need you to maintain my cover. Can you do that for me?"

"Sure, what's going on?"

Without going into too much detail, Clay explained to Ballard what had happened in Vietnam with the Bac Thu organization and their efforts to neutralize him and Gary Baker. They followed Cherry determined to use her to get to us. She's now somewhere in the US I don't know where. Baker is somewhere unknown as well. The FBI is around me all the time and is in my ear, literally in my ear.

They set me up with this cover. I decided to use it to get out of the apartment and see the country and maybe run into Cherry somewhere. We travel to these venues like yours and perform for the crowd and make a big deal out of Veterans everywhere we go. Anything we make over our expenses we donate to local Veterans centers. We try to make them feel appreciated in this small way.

Many of them don't know what treatments are available to them for their situations or where to get them. We scout out the best and closest locations and share that with the spectators who may be in need or know someone that does.

You can help us help them by keeping my secret. I'm running this project until next summer. Hopefully the CIA has done their thing by then. We have a lot of fun doing this but it does get crowded in the bus sometimes. Is there anywhere close we can get showered up before the performance or actually after the races since the usual dirt and exhaust fumes are all over us by then."

"Wow that's quite a story Clay. I have a small hotel in town that would work just fine for you guys. My ranch is just outside of town and were having a big barbeque for the drivers and mechanics tonight, you're welcome to come. When we're done here follow me over to the ranch and we can chill and you can see my collection of farm animals."

"Sounds great Ballard, I let the guys know."

They went back outside to the bus, Clay let them know what was going on. The guys were really excited about the Hotel and the barbeque.

Bud fired up the bus and followed Ballard's pickup out to the ranch. They piled out and went around to the back of the house and found some sweet tea on tap, next to the swimming pool.

Ballard and Clay wandered over to the corral and looked out over the landscape.

"This is beautiful country Ballard," said Clay. "What all kinds of animals do you have here?"

"We have some Buffalo over on the east range, some Long Horns over on the west range and just south of here we raise a large herd of Angus for sale. We use the Buffalo for tourists, we have a lot of call to run the Long Horns on western days event in towns around here. Don't worry the cows are tame and could probably find their own way around some of those places they've been there so many times.

We also have an assortment of wild life that keeps things interesting as well. Aside from the rattlers there are bobcats, and even a mountain lion or two have been spotted. Skunks, Opossums, Armadillos, and such provide fare for the local Road Kill café.

"Oh my God are you kidding me?" blurted out Clay.

"Yes, Clay I'm kidding. That one gets the tourists every time."

"This is impressive Ballard. I hope to have a small farm in the mid-west after this is all over."

"I heard about your buddy Wallace at Cam Ranh in the rocket attack. That guy deserves a Silver Star or a Medal of Honor."

"He sure does. That was a rough day. He could have run for cover anytime and I wouldn't have thought anything about it. I took a bump on the head but after a couple days in the med tent I was ok.

About that time there was a ruckus out front of the house. Piper was guarding the bus as usual and was going on like a crazy dog. We ran around the side of the house just in time to see a large Diamond Back rattler take a shot at him. He must have struck him as he ran off yelping.

About the time I thought this day couldn't get any weirder an Eagle swooped down out of nowhere and snatched that snake up and disappeared into the western sun. We caught up with Piper on his fourth trip around the bus. Bud grabbed him and the first aid kit and started administering some antiseptic. Ballard ran into the house and came out with a syringe of anti-venom suitable for animals.

"He's not the first critter to get into a tussle with a rattler around here. "Nature has its way of dealing with nature." Said Ballard. As we watched the Eagle disappear into the sunset.

"He should be ok in an hour or so. Just let him rest over by the pool during dinner. You guys might even play some guitar music for the guests in a few.

They all went back and relaxed by the pool. The barbeque sure smelled good. The rest of the guests were starting to arrive. This was going to be quite a party.

"Before you go Clay, I met your dad up in Ohio a few weeks ago. Your mom and Cherry were there for an FAC Memorial ceremony. They are anxious to see you. Cherry looks just like she did they day I met with her in Da Nang. The authorities need to get this over with.

That next evening the Band played opening sets while the patrons arrived at the track and during the intermission. When it was over, they loaded up and drove over to the Hotel and settled in for the night.

"Whew...what a day huh," Clay mumbled to Piper. "You going to be ok there fella?"

Piper raised his head and gave him one of his cool stares, signifying that of course he was going to be ok. He even wagged his tail for a few seconds.

It was good to see Ballard again.

Spring was setting in and the chance of thunderstorms and all the trimmings that come with it were a daily nuisance. We managed to miss the crux of it. Dodged a couple of tornadoes in West Texas and a hail storm with stones the size of small plates in Oklahoma. We drove through one small town after a storm had passed and witnessed what ten minutes of violent weather can do. We stopped and helped pull people out of collapsed houses and stores. God bless those folks.

Time after time I thought I saw red stingrays, or girls with white hair. Time after time I was disappointed. Bud knew I was looking for something but he kept it too himself...for now.

We played a couple of gigs somewhere out in the middle of nowhere, we had to hang around for a few days because the 'Bean' had some issues with the brakes. I must confess some places are more hospitable than others. Some just give you the creeps. We needed to move on as soon as possible.

We played a few 'Honkey Tonks' in Arizona and actually got an invite to play a casino in Vegas. Everybody was super excited about that. I told them not to get too overboard, it was a pretty small casino. Regardless, they are beside themselves with glee. Maybe it was because we would get to sleep in a hotel with hot running water, clean sheets, toilets, TVs, and something to eat other than pizza.

We pulled into the parking lot, Bud and Piper started looking for a place to park the bus. Piper keeps unwanted guests away, that dog can show his teeth and scare even the biggest of them away.

A young lady came out to meet us and told Bud where he could park. She introduced herself and gave us cards to get into our rooms. Cindy was on her name tag.

I said, "Cindy...what's good to eat around here close by?"

She started spieling off name after name, my head started to spin so I called for a time out. "Steak, where can I get a good steak?"

She gave us directions to a good restaurant close by. We checked into the hotel, got cleaned up and met back for a walk to dinner.

None of us had ever been to Vegas. It was all glittery and everything. Cindy warned us to stay close by as there are some tough areas of town. No sense in testing the waters on that.

We played our sets the next day and got a pretty good response. The owner liked what he heard and saw. I had introduced my new invention, laser holographs. I could holograph just about anything from additional band mates to dancing girls to fireworks. Bud got a kick out of running the thing while we played.

After a week or so we were attracting quite a crowd. The owner even gave us a bonus. The guys loved that. I had to pay the bus with mine. The jelly bean was in need of some TLC while we're in one spot.

I scanned the audience for any sign of younger white-haired girls. There are indeed quite a few white-haired ladies, if you know what I mean.

Between sets one evening, I thought I smelled that Heavenly perfume. The FBI guy told me to not worry about it.

We had a good time, made some friends, some cash and even came up with a couple of original tunes. Some producer caught up with us and we made a demo and sure enough it cracked the top 100 at 99. Stayed there for a couple of weeks. The guys are so excited.

I was getting into a funk, tired and anxious to get on with my life, hopefully with Cherry, if she'll still have me.

The weather was turning warmer so we started turning back north and east. First, we're going to hit a shopping mall in Salt Lake, then on over toward Denver, and then our last stop, Terra Haute.

Only the bus would never make it to Terra Haute.

Chapter Twenty-One

"What's that wig for?" asked Cherry to Agent Renfroe.

"You'll see, let's go do some shopping tonight, it'll be fun. I think you need some time out for a while. You'll love it, we can get some ice cream."

"I'm not really in the mood, I've had a hard day at work, I just want to lay down for a while."

"Come on," said Renfroe, "this is not an option today. Get your face on, wear some of that fancy perfume, and put on that wig."

"Ugg...but I don't want too." Whined Cherry.

Renfroe gave her a stern steely eyed stare. "Come on."

"Oh...ok."

Renfroe drove them over to the local shopping mall. They parked, got out, and went inside.

"What is that god awful racket?" Sneered Cherry.

"I don't know," said Renfroe, "let's go check it out."

They walked towards the sound and surprisingly it got more musical and actually sounded pretty good the closer they got. There were a lot of young people standing around kinda dancing to the music.

Cherry curiously peaked over the railing to see what the fuss was all about. There was a sign hanging behind the musicians that read, "Clay Carter and the Snake Skin Rangers" she caught her breath. She turned to Renfroe, "Is that?"

"Yes, it is."

Cherry started bawling like a baby calf. The lady next to them just smiled and said, "Well, I thought they were pretty good, don't you?"

Renfroe spoke to her and told her she just really liked the Clay guy. She'll be ok.

Cherry choked back tears and squeezed Renfroe's hand till she screeched in pain.

"Ow, she squeaked. You're hurting me."

Cherry trembled and cooed softly along with the music.

"That was one of our favorite songs."

Clay bellowed into the microphone, "That one was for a very special lady out there somewhere, think good thoughts my love, good thoughts."

Renfroe had to drag her away as they still had to remain undercover for the near future.

"This will be over soon Cherry. I've heard some good things from headquarters. Rainy season is over and they're closing in.

Cherry gushed over and over, "Thank you, thank you so much, thank you."

Chapter Twenty-Two

Dan and Martha had kept up with RJ in the trade magazines as well as regular reports from the FBI concerning him and Cherry. The two young people are hanging on, but they are weary and in need of a break. The rest of the family could use a break as well.

The Lazy J was steady and had many new customers especially since a new truck stop went in across the road. The grandparents are slowly retiring from the restaurant business and young folks are filling the spots. Martha's parents had lived near them for the last twenty-five years and have decided to move into a new assisted living center nearby.

Tom was busy flying commercial jets; he has some new aircraft types to fly. New fly by wire technology was the big thing now. He had a chance to see RJ and the Snake Skin Rangers play outside of Denver this past week.

Lanora was busy with her children and school. Husband Daren works for an oil company and they are doing pretty well.

"I think I might try to catch RJ in concert up in Terra Haute next week before the journeys end, said Dan, wanna come with me?" He asked.

Martha replied, "Sure, it's not too far. The restaurants in good hands."

Dan and Martha made the trip to Terra Haute, found a decent motel and waited for RJ's bus to arrive. After a few days of waiting Dan went to investigate the situation.

Dan nervously opened the door to the motel where Martha was waiting inside.

"I checked with the speedway manager. The bus never arrived and he's not heard anything. He said he would give us a call if anything changed.

Martha looked at him with dread in her eyes, her face drawn.

"I just saw something on the TV news. There was an RV out in the middle of nowhere, burning, its tires shot out. There was no sign of life. The police were interviewed and said the investigation is ongoing. I couldn't tell if it was RJ's bus or not. Dan I'm so scared."

Dan sat down beside her, he thought, this means something, he just didn't know what.

"Let's not jump to any conclusions...ok."

Chapter Twenty-Three

The radio crackled into the ear piece, "base to 1-1, do you copy?"

"Copy base, this is 1-1, go ahead."

"We have a swift boat tracking one of Bac's pirate ships. They are keeping a safe distance and watching them on radar."

"Roger base, what's the next step?"

"Rendezvous at site Charlie. We need to discuss what we know."

"Copy Base, 1-1 out."

Later that day several operatives, known only by their call sign, gathered together at site Charlie, somewhere off the coast of Cambodia.

One person, apparently the leader started laying out maps.

"This is where we think their terminal is. They use what looks like legitimate shipping to cover for their trafficking, they also use their pirate ships to ward off anyone curious. We followed one of the pirate ships to the location on the map here." He points to a spot where a river empties into the ocean.

"We have an agent inside the organization that's going to send up infrared strobe signals as they follow the traffic up river to the inland operations.

We have someone on this oil rig here. We have someone on one of their ships. There are several operatives spread throughout the organization from the gun running, to human traffic and so on.

We are working to get to the bottom of why they targeted the airmen. So far it appears that the caravan that got shot up was loaded with hi-tech electronics. Seismic equipment for Oil exploration and mining. The most advanced computer tech for researching the best drug manufacturing methods. It had sophisticated surveillance equipment for spying on government and industry. The hit set them back years.

We are going to insert someone close to the head office to locate the main computer terminal and insert a floppy disk with a virus on it that will erase any trace of the airmen.

Any illegal activity that we find we will give the details to the regional governments. The locals cannot be trusted. The regional directors might not be either.

The plan is to do small sabotage and theft. Nothing too big, just enough to keep them occupied and confused.

We have also determined that while there are some leaders, each division of their operation has its own heads. The eye-opening thing was that Bac Thu isn't one person. It's a network of tribes that operate separate from one another. They still network and report financially to a central office location.

We have an operative working with a supply train to locate that head office. Progress has been very slow. There are many sub camps along the way, each has its own tributaries for incoming and outgoing products and people. Our operative has followed the wrong one twice and had to back track. Her efforts must pay off soon as our tech is aging and it may or may not be effective by the time, she gets it to the main network.

We have satellite and U-2 surveillance but that is not very effective due to the forest canopy they operate under. We sent out high level surveillance aircraft and have been able to follow the IR strobes. Right now, they are going in circles.

Our physical sabotage and communication disruption activities are starting to get results. Our voice traffic has monitored some pretty intense conversations from several locations."

The operative on the Oil rig, call sign 'eager 4' reported today.

"Base this is E-4, do you read?"

"Loud and clear E-4, send traffic."

"Small generator fire, stopped up sewer lines, broken antenna for radio, food spoiled due to refrigeration not working. Workers are irritated and starting to grumble. Management is confused but not aware the incidents are sabotage as yet. Going to lay low for a while. E-4 out."

The operative on the freighter reported yesterday. Call sign, S-2.

"S-2 calling Base, how copy?"

"Five by five S-2, send traffic."

"Engines are getting bad fuel. Starting to crude up. Water supply fouled and stinks. Radios have bad tubes and have lost power. Number two cargo hold is leaking severely. Crew having to move cargo from one hold to another. Crew is testy and getting rebellious. Management is getting suspicious. May have to jump to another ship for a time. S-2 out."

"Our ground operative is due to report in tomorrow. Hopefully she's found the right trail this time."

The ground operative is checking in now. Call sign, M-3.

"M-3 calling base, how copy?"

"Clear M-3, send traffic."

"Have sighted a caravan with equipment marked fragile. The human trafficking trains are going to a camp marked on the map at coordinates x-ray 21-27. They are then split up and sent to cities for prostitution or enslavement. The guns are going to a different camp trail marked z-9 on the map. They are intended for some terrorist organization operating out of Africa. The drugs are in a chemical state at this point and are headed to a manufacturing plant for processing at map coordinates BR-AB.

I'm following the cargo marked fragile, IR strobes active. M-3 out."

Ok that's news for the Regional Directors to follow up on. Hopefully it will distract Bac's people long enough for M-3 to get access to the main terminal.

The following week, the operatives commandeered one of the pirate ships. Replacing all the crew with friendlies.

"Let's get all their intel back to base," said the leader.

"We're going to use this vessel to slip into the main harbor and plant mines in strategic areas that will weaken their defenses and slow operations down. The problem we are having is there are a great many locals that work for the organization that are considered civilians. We don't want to go around killing anyone. This has got to be surgical. A water line here, an electrical station there. An empty boat or two. Pipe for the oil rig with the threads all twisted."

So far voice traffic has them searching for answers on the oil rig and the freighter. One of the camps used for human trafficking got raided and shut down for now. That tribe scattered far and wide. It won't take them long to recover but it has them scratching their heads.

"Ahn, get over here and help Tat with the equipment."

Ahn, aka, M-3, complied.

"Load that crate onto the barge, that crate over there goes onto the truck. The smaller boxes go onto the bikes for the trail to Bac Thu headquarters. I need you to go with the barge."

"Yes, Hahn, but I could be more help with the bikes, I am strong and slender. I can get into tight spaces easy; I also am in good shape for the journey."

Hahn thought for a minute, "Ok" he said, "go with the bikes. That equipment is very fragile, do not drop it."

Ahn, replied, "Yes I will be very careful."

She gathered her personal items and stuffed them into her backpack. She was on the right trail this time, she was sure. She set the IR strobe and worked her way to the back of the line where she could observe carefully where they're going.

There was a mix of male and female workers pushing the bikes up the hills and through the jungle. The trail got very narrow at times, pushing her skills to their limits.

They would stop every few hours for a rest break, and make camp at dusk. They are well fed and have plenty of fresh water. She tracked their progress on a small map she had tucked away in her pack. The IR strobe signaled the overhead aircraft the location of the caravan.

Back at headquarters they're celebrating the progress made in the interdiction efforts. One of the ships was sunk, the Oil rig was nearly useless with bad pipe. Some of the chemicals for drugs had been adulterated making that batch a waste. M-3 was on a trail never seen from the air or mapping satellites before. The U-2 using infrared radar spotted a large settlement about fifty klicks to the northwest of where the IR strobes are flashing.

M-3 was carving some new intelligence out of the wilderness. So far so good.

Operatives in the cities had tracked some of the human trafficking victims and got them released and returned to their homes.

Bac Thu's presence in the region was beginning to show weakness. They are scrambling to plug leaks and find saboteurs. We had been very careful and didn't move on anyone area too quickly. Many of the problems are explainable by simple personnel attrition and mechanical fatigue. It's tough to maintain an illegal trade operation twenty-four-seven twelve months out of the year without episode. That's what we're counting on.

So far Bac's people haven't suspected any one person for the incidents. We must keep it that way and get all our own people back safe as well.

Locals are easily bought for small tasks. You can basically get someone offed for a fiver, if that's what you wanted done. We didn't want anyone offed, just confused and dismayed. None of our fingerprints could be on any part of this, operation now called, "Operation Boil the Frog."

Slowly but surely to twist and turn them, I believe they call that "Gas Lighting." We are going to Gas Light the heck out of them so they leave the US and our airmen alone forever. They must become and remain forgetful.

We had other operations going on in this theater of operations as well. There are plenty of evil tyrants and drug lords to go around. This Bac organization is just one of many.

Hopefully we can close the door on Bac, and trap some others in their own web of destruction.

Suddenly the IR strobes from M-3 stopped about thirty klicks from the large heat source we had already identified. That's a huge concern.

Oh my, Ahn thought to herself, I wonder how long the IR strobe hasn't been working? She did some troubleshooting and found a battery had come loose. "Oh, thank goodness she murmured."

The IR strobe back on, she worried about where they're going. The trail suddenly opened up to a road wide enough for trucks. She needed to stay with the equipment regardless of where or how it moved. She started playing herself up as a technical specialist to convince the leader that she might be useful at some future tasks.

They met some trucks at the trail head. Everyone and everything were loaded into the trucks. They travelled the remaining fifteen klicks by truck. When they got to their destination there was a flurry of activity. As best she could determine there had been some major disruptions in the operations. Leaders are franticly trying to determine the source of their problems.

The leader of this group scurried around and had everyone unloading and staging the equipment in a warehouse location. It was heavily guarded with armed personnel everywhere.

Ahn was going to have to slip past the guards to load the floppy disk into the main computer. For now, she had to blend in with the workers running around trying to stay out of trouble.

Headquarters was back online with the IR strobe from M-3. It had stopped at a location and hadn't moved for two days. This appears to be the main hub of activity. We plan to create some distractions so she can get her mission accomplished.

Ahn sent some morse IR signals requesting some supplies. She needed some way to put some people temporarily to sleep. Preferably not injectables, just dermatological touch agents she could apply to their skin or something they were going to touch, like a keyboard or a canteen.

We helicoptered an agent in about two klicks away and he hiked in overnight. They were able to meet on the outskirts of the encampment and trade supplies and information.

In the meantime, our campaign of Gas Lighting was beginning to work wonders. The various districts are running out of supplies and information was sketchy. They were chasing their tails. The pot was beginning to get a little hotter.

Ahn signaled by IR laser that the next night she was going to attempt entry into the main office. A few guards are going to need a nap and one of them needed to provide a key to the front door.

The guards would never know what hit them and wouldn't remember a thing. What laid in wait behind door number one was the big mystery.

Ahn made a trial run to see how well the anesthetic worked, and how long it lasted. She put a few of the outer level guards down for a nap. It worked perfectly. She waited to see how long it lasted. She hoped for at least an hour maybe two. What she got was a very rough forty-five minutes. The results varied from one person to another based on their size.

She was going to have to streamline her approach and simplify the point of entry. Maybe there is a way in from the roof? She had to gain interior access or the whole op was a bust. She also needed to get out alive.

Looks like the roof access through the vents is the best way in. Let's rope down and see whose home, shall we.

Chapter Twenty-Four

"I'm a whole lot more than RJ's girlfriend. A whole lot more. I have a career, the people I work with like me. I make good decisions. I work well with others." Fumed Cherry.

"What's going on girl?" Asked Renfroe.

"I don't know, I just feel penned up here all of a sudden. Like there is no me, just RJ's girlfriend."

"Oh my gosh what brought all this on? You are where you chose to be. You could pick a different place anytime you want. And you're right. People like you; you have a great career and fantastic reputation. You are your own person."

"There's a world out there, I want to see it and experience it without skulking around like a bandit."

"Oh," said Renfroe, "you need a vacation."

"What's a vacation," quizzed Cherry.

"You've never been on a vacation?" Said Renfroe, surprised.

"No, I haven't, what do you do on a 'vacation."

"Well, you can go to a different town, city, state, or a park, a museum, camping, boating, fishing, or in winter you can go to the mountains and ski. You could go to the ocean, the beach and swim or just soak up some sun."

"I guess I saw RJ just moving around the country just willy nilly, 'all exaggerated' I got a bit jealous. Where is the nearest ocean beach," she asked.

"I will arrange for a trip to a California beach at the earliest possible time. You can wear that swim suit you bought at the mall the other day."

"California here we come," yelled Cherry, "woohoo."

They arrived at a beach near Ventura. They walked the lane of shops and watched the people go up and down the pier. She wanted to ride the big Ferris wheel so they did that. They rented a big umbrella and some beach chairs, found a spot and watched the sun move across the sky.

"This is wonderful," cooed Cherry. "Thanks, Renfroe. You know how to put on a vacation."

After the sun started to wane, the two of them went back to their hotel and cleaned up. Dressing up for dinner was a real treat. They found a nice restaurant on the strip and ordered some seafood.

"I haven't had fresh seafood in forever, mentioned Renfroe. This is really good. How is yours Cherry." She asked.

"I've had Maine lobster and crab all my life from the east coast. This is different and quite good. I think of home quite often. The trees and the deep blue ocean. We have beaches there also. This is more like a carnival atmosphere here, it's quite entertaining."

The week progressed nicely as they visited venues for sight-seeing. Even renting a car and driving along the coastal highway. The weather was beautiful and the drive spectacular.

Alas the week came to an end. The two of them packed and went to the airport for the flight back to Utah.

Cherry thought that she could get used to this vacation business.

"I will plan for a vacation every year and go someplace different every time.

I hear there is a grand amusement park in Anaheim, I would like to go there someday," she dreamed out loud.

Cherry got back in the swing of things with a better frame of mind. It's good to recharge the batteries you know.

Agent Renfroe said, "Hey, how about we go up skiing this next weekend before the season is over? What do you think?"

"Sounds good to me. Another shopping trip, eh?"

"Yes, another shopping trip," quipped Renfroe.

They loaded up on all kinds of cold weather gear, caps, gloves, snow bunny suits, all the ski stuff. They wanted to look good after all. They got fitted for their rental equipment, it would be delivered to their rooms when they got to the resort.

That Friday evening, they drove up to a ski resort in the Wasatch mountains. It was a beautiful drive and the resort was quite comfortable and pleasant with a big huge fireplace with a crackling fire. The restaurant was very good with a variety of cuisine to choose from besides the usual fast-food fare. They chose to have adjoining suites for this trip, each with a different view of the mountain range.

The next morning the pair ventured off to the pro shop to get their lift tickets. They were ready for a day on the slopes. Agent Renfroe was still working and was vigilant about all their surroundings. Agent Smith hung out in the lodge scanning for any unsavory characters. Cherry was ready to have some fun.

They finished getting into their outfits and went outside. They caught the next lift to the mid-range difficulty slopes. The runs were not overly crowded as it was near the end of the season. Still there were plenty of people of all ages enjoying themselves. The sun was out and there were some shinny spots where it had melted and refrozen. Both Cherry and Marsha called them out to each other to pay special attention, especially on the west side of any trail where the sun had shone the previous day.

They glided gracefully down the trail the breeze blowing softly and the sun shining on their faces. The trail narrowed occasionally which required some vigilance for traffic. The runs were mostly open but several were also tree lined. The pair went to the bottom and caught the lift back up to catch a more difficult run. They exited the lift chair just as a couple of kids ages twelve or thirteen went zipping past them.

The run was a factor or two more difficult but they handled it easily. Cherry was really enjoying the day out. Agent Renfroe obviously needed a change of scenery herself.

They came to a part of the trail that was especially steep and both spotted some shiny spots.

"Whoa there Cherry," said Renfroe. "This is a nasty looking patch of ground."

They slowed to a crawl, snow plowing their way past the icy patch. Just then Renfroe called out.

"Look over there, down the side of the hill, what is that? It looks like a couple of bodies."

Cherry slowly ventured over to the edge and looked carefully down the hill. "Oh my God Renfroe it is a couple of bodies. It looks like the two kids that went speeding past us earlier."

Cherry popped off her skis and side stepped down the hill to the first of the kids. She was unconscious and appeared to be suffering from impact injuries to her head, face and torso. She was bleeding profusely from a broken arm that had bones protruding. Cherry quickly assessed the damage and started ripping off pieces of her clothing to triage the wounds. She checked her vital signs. Her pulse was weak and breathing very shallow. Clearly struggling to breath, she may have broken ribs.

Cherry got the arm wound wrapped and splinted with a couple of handy branches. Renfroe yelled down that she was going after the ski patrol. She tossed her back pack down the hill to Cherry. Renfroe always had stuff in her pack for first aid situations. Cherry got the girl stabilized and slowly slid her sideways down the hill back to the trail.

She went back to check the condition of the boy. His injuries were substantial and different as well. His pelvis was out of position and one ankle was clearly broken. His head was covered in blood and he had a pretty good-sized dent. He most certainly had a concussion on top of the other injuries.

She found the wound on his head and wrapped gauze from the kit to contain the blood flow. His pelvis and ankle were serious and needed major treatment as soon as possible. His vitals were very weak and his eyes not responding well. She did her best to make him comfortable and slowly started to slide him towards the trail. Just about the time she got him out of the woods the ski patrol showed up with a pair of snow plows and a horde of medical personnel.

Cherry detailed each of the kids' injuries to the paramedics to the best of her ability. They took over and got each of them on IV's and oxygen. There was a helicopter waiting at the bottom of the hill.

"Do you want a ride down the hill miss? Asked one of the drivers.

"No thanks, I think I will just collect my skis and make my own way down. You guys have the situation well in hand. Be off with you."

Cherry went back up the hill to her equipment. Got her skis back on and slowly made her way down the hill. She thought surely the resort has a way to warn skiers of potential slick spots. Maybe they just missed that one.

Cherry met up with Renfroe at the lodge and sat down for a mug of hot chocolate.

"Well, we've had quite the day. Apparently those two kids will be in hospital for a while but they should be ok thanks to your quick thinking and trauma skills. The parents want us to come over to their home when we get back to the city for a dinner. I think he is a U.S. Senator or something like that."

"Ok well, for the moment I need to just settle my nerve make one more run up the hill before we call it a day. Is that ok with you?

"Sure," said Renfroe. "Let's do it."

The rest of the day was uneventful. They really enjoyed the big crackling fire in the lodge and even roasted some marshmallows before turning in.

"That was quite the experience wasn't it Renfroe? I'm actually glad we came up and I have no regrets. I'm curious about the parents though, could we send Agent Smith in my place?"

"I don't think so Cherry, not this time."

The next week after everything had settled back into the usual routines Renfroe knocked on Cherries apartment door and informed her of the plans to go to the home of the kids they helped out on the ski slope.

"Do I look ok for this; I haven't done formal stuff in a while."

"You look great. Just be you it will be fine."

They pulled up in the driveway of a four-story mansion. An attendant opened their doors for them and parked the car.

"Welcome ladies, dinner will be in a couple of hours. We would like to get acquainted first before we dine. I'm Mrs. Arthur and this is my husband the honorable Senator Jess Arthur. We have other guests coming tonight as well.

Your name is Cherry Wilson is that correct?"

"Yes, it is."

"And what are we to call you miss...?"

"I'm Agent Marsha Renfroe with the FBI office out of California."

"So, are you guys' friends or something?"

"You could say that."

Agent Renfroe grinned and moved the conversation along.

"How are your children doing? They had quite a tumble up there."

"Well, each of them is going to be ok, it will be some time before they are mobile. Teddy has a concussion and broken pelvis and ankle. He has a bit of amnesia right now and has no recollection of what happened. Karen is on a respirator but is healing up.

"If you don't mind my asking, how do you know how to do what you did Cherry?"

"I'm a nurse, I just got back from a tour of duty in Australia and South Vietnam as a first line US Airforce Captain trauma nurse.

"Oh...Vietnam. I expect that might have been difficult for you." The hostess said rather smugly.

"You have no idea. The young people of this nation stepped up and did their duty in service to this country and have been treated very poorly for it. I hope as a government official you can correct some of the mistreatment they've endured."

"Well Miss Cherry, we are so thankful for the extra special treatment you gave our children that day on the mountain. Because of your efforts we believe they will be back to their old selves in no time."

"You're welcome from the bottom of my heart Senator and Mrs. Arthur. But know this, all children are special to me. There are no extra special ones. They are extra special to you as they should be. To me all children are just as special as the next one."

Cherry and Agent Renfroe made the best of the rest of the evening's festivities. Cherry whispered to Marsha. "I'm not cut out for this kind of stuff. This is more painful that basic training. Let's make our exit as soon as possible."

"Before you go ladies, I would like to ask you to come to Washington someday soon and educate the Congress on how they can better serve our men and women in uniform and our Veterans. Would you be up for that Miss Cherry?"

"After I complete my current project, I would be happy to make a trip to Washington. We can make those arrangements then. Good day to you sir and best wishes for your family and their recovery."

"Whew, can we please get out of here Marsha?"

Marsha just giggled and slammed the car door.

"We should have had Agent Smith do this. I'm sure my foot is firmly placed in my mouth. It may take me weeks to get all the shoe polish off my face. Let's go get some ice cream.

"So," popped off Renfroe, "how about we go horseback riding next weekend, how's that sound?"

The silence was deafening.

Chapter Twenty-Five

"Martha," said Dan. "I just heard from the Speedway in Terry Haute. He says that the guys stayed longer in the Boulder area. Seems a big-name promoter wanted them to do a series of concerts at a local amphitheater. He also wanted them to open for some of the better-known acts.

They're going to hang out there for several days. Terry Haute is still the last stop on their tour. He said he would give us a call when they arrived."

"Oh, thank you Dan, I worried that something awful had happened. I'm going over to the church this afternoon. There is a yard sale going on to benefit one of the families that lost their son. I'm going to help out for a while. I will be back for dinner."

While Martha was out Dan got on the phone with his CIA contact for an update.

"Hello Dan, how are you doing?"

"Well, I'd be doing a lot better if you had some good news for me. Can you tell me what's the status of the operation?"

"As you know I can't divulge too much information but I can tell you this. We've been waging a campaign of minor disturbances to distract the organization while our main operative gains access to the central hub of the operation. They have sited its location and are surveying the best access points to get inside the cage where the critical paper and electronic information is stored.

We have a team waiting just outside the perimeter. So far there appears to be one individual that stays inside the cage. I say cage, it's a box like a train car size wrapped in foil type material to make it a faraday cage. Nothing goes in or out by airwaves. It's all transmitted by a T-1 trunk line. We are working to find the connection to the cage and tap it. It is heavily guarded and well hidden.

Our operative has found a way in through the vents in the roof. They will rope down and see who's in there within the next couple of days. Once we have gained entry and the T-1 trunk line is exposed, the team will tap it. We will send false messages to all the Bac suppliers and customers telling them that the Bac organization is blown. All the incoming and outgoing transaction details have been sent to the government along with names and addresses of buyers and dealers.

Then they will ping the line with a high voltage spike and fry whatever electronics are inside the cage. Any intel left on paper will be collected and carried off or burned. The guy inside captured and interred forever.

RJ, Lt. Baker, and anyone associated with them will no longer be an item for anyone to harass.

The timeline on the final step is 2100 hours on the fifteenth of this month. Just a couple of days away.

Hold your breath Dan, this isn't done yet, but we're very close."

"Thanks, we pray for this to have a successful conclusion. Dan out."

When Martha returned that evening Dan shared a condensed version of the latest news. She was overjoyed at the prospect of this whole dilemma ending soon.

Chapter Twenty-Six

"Hey Bud, what's the deal with the promoter?" Asked Clay.

"He heard us play in Salt Lake and thought we would be a good fit for his summer series of concerts. There are several venues some larger than others. Couple of them are large amphitheater outdoor areas, and a couple are indoor arenas. The money is good. It will vary based on the size of the venue and crowd. As for the indoor arenas, we will get a percent of the ticket sales. He has us tentatively booked for three weeks. Depending of course, on everyone's approval."

"What does Piper think?" chuckled Clay.

"Oh well, he's all in. There are some great dog parks around here. He's having a blast."

"Where are we staying? I hope it's nice, my back is in need of a regular size bed and a regular size shower."

"It's a suite hotel in Boulder, close to all the locations where we're going to be performing. I thought I'd try my hand at some backup rhythm guitar the next few outings." Said Bud.

"Are you any good," said Clay? "Play something for me, I want to hear what you've got."

"Ok, I can do that."

Bud pulled out an old beat-up guitar he'd found at a pawn shop. Tuned it and started strumming.

"She's not too purty but she sounds really mellow." Remarked Bud.

Bud strummed the guitar and started to hum a tune from one of the songs that was in their program. Clay pulled out his twelve string and started playing along.

"Hey," Bud said. "That sounds really good."

They started singing the lyrics and next thing they knew they were drawing a small crowd.

They got some lawn chairs out of the hold in the bus set them up and started playing for the crowd.

Someone in the gathering asked, "Hey, you take requests?"

"Depends on the request," Clay hollered back. "What do you want to hear?"

The audience member hollered out his request.

"I think we can do that," said Clay.

Bud and Clay played on for about an hour. The other band mates had gone shopping for some new clothes before the next set of performances.

"Hey you guys sound pretty good. We could hear you all the way across the parking lot."

Bud and Clay continued to play and sing for a few more minutes.

"Sorry folks it's getting dinner time. Come out to one of our concerts in the next few days and you can hear the whole band."

They all piled into the pickup truck and headed over to one of the famous steak houses for dinner.

They ordered their meals and drank coffee or some soda. Clay was not big on alcohol. If the guys wanted to drink beer or something, they did it away from Clay.

Nick the drummer spoke up, "This next couple of weeks will be fun. Stay in one spot for a time. I sense we're about done though don't you think Clay." He asked.

"After we do the Terra Haute speedway gig, we're heading back to Springfield and disbanding." Said Clay. "I've done my traveling fun. We have a good size bank account to split when we get there and then you guys can go your own way. It's been a pleasure and an honor to play with you guys. Honestly, I thought this was going to be huge disappointment in the beginning and then poof, like magic it all came together."

As we were leaving a young lady came up me and asked for my autograph.

"Ok, no problem," I said.

She kind of stood there afterward and acted like she wanted something else.

"Is there something else miss," queried Clay? "We're on our way out the door."

She acted like she wanted to come with us.

"Sorry miss, we have a tight squeeze in the truck," said Bud. Coming to the rescue. She was not the first young lady that wanted to make a move in their direction. Clay was clearly not interested; the other guys could do what they do on their own time.

They checked into the hotel for the night, tomorrow was a big day in a big arena.

The next morning Clay awoke and thought he heard voices in the next room. He couldn't make out what they were saying but they sounded really intense.

"I need a cup of coffee." He mumbled to himself.

He knocked on Bud's room door. Bud answered and Piper greeted him with a toothy grin.

"Come on Piper, let's go get a cup of coffee."

Clay and Piper made their way down to the lobby. Clay poured himself a big cup of coffee and he and Piper went out to the yard where Piper chased butterflies for a few minutes. Clay pulled out the snap shot of Cherry and ran his thumb over the picture to wipe off the pocket fuzz.

"Piper, what do you think man. Will I ever see her again?"

Piper paused and looked at him as if he understood, and gave him another one of his toothy grins.

"I think that dog knows something," muttered Clay. Maybe he's an Angel too. Piper wheeled around and stared at him.

"Come on Piper, let's go for a walk."

"Don't wander too far off." Spoke the voice in his ear.

"Hey how you doing today Agent...Agent...what's your name again?"

"You will never know my name Clay."

"Well, what if I wanted to invite you to my wedding someday."

"If, you get married, and again I say if, I will be there and you will never know its me."

"Oh, that sounds…"

Just then a car backfired in the road next to the hotel, both Piper and Clay ducked into the bushes. After a few minutes they emerged from their hiding place, as an elderly couple was passing by on the sidewalk.

Thinking fast he explained, "We lost a bone in the bushes and had to dig around to find it."

The pair gave them a strange look and hurried on their way.

"Come on boy let's get back, I'm starved, let's go get some breakfast." Piper trotted off like he owned the sidewalk. Clay followed obediently.

That evening after the concert they returned to the Hotel and parked the bus. Everyone clambered out, except Clay.

They hollered at him to come on. "I'm going to hang here for a few minutes. I need to go over the vitals on the bus and top off some fluids."

"Ok," they hollered back, "don't be too long though."

Clay checked around the bus briefly and then grabbed a lawn chair and climbed up to the roof of the bus. He reclined the chair and laid there looking up at the stars. In the thin mountain air, the stars were like a cloud. You felt like you could almost reach out and touch them.

There were a few shooting stars and there goes a satellite. Mostly it was quiet and peaceful. His thoughts of course wandered toward home, and his beloved Cherry Wilson. He also wondered where his stingray was. He took the FBI out of his ear for a few moments.

"I pray Lord, you are most gracious and loving. Please guide us back together again safe and sound."

The setting was so serene that he fell asleep on the roof of the bus.

"Where the heck is he," yelled Nick. "Ed, have you seen Clay, he missed bed check. The FBI guy is frantic."

"No, I haven't seen him. I was busy sleeping. Where could he have gotten off too?"

"I don't know. I'm going to the lobby to see if he's down there getting coffee. You and Zane go check the bus, that's where he was last night."

"I've been all over the grounds and all around the bus," said Zane. "There's no sign of him in his room, the bus, the grounds, surely, he didn't meet up with someone. Nah that's not like him. Does the hotel have camera's anywhere?"

The group went down to hotel security and woke up the guard. Some guard. "Hey aren't you supposed to be awake?!" Chorused the group.

"Oh...hey can I help you with something?"

"Yeah, our band mate has vanished. We're wondering if you have any camera footage we can look at?"

"Sure, it's right here."

There were about six or so video screens all blank at the moment.

"Oh sorry. I forget to turn on the monitors. There you go, you can check the surroundings and the roof."

"The roof, we forgot the roof."

"Somebody needs to go up and check the roof."

They scanned back at the evening footage and never saw Clay enter the lobby; he must still be in the parking lot. Scanning forwards there's no footage of him ever coming in.

They radioed the guard on the roof.

"Ok, anything on the roof? I've already called the authorities; they're going to conduct an all-out search."

Sirens came blaring in from all directions. Lights flashing, vehicles surrounded the hotel. Guests were starting to emerge looking a bit concerned. Management calmed them down ensuring them there was no immediate threat to their safety.

Just then the radio crackled, "Hey you guys, I'm up here on the roof of the hotel, I found him."

"Holy smoke, thank God. Where is he?"

"He's asleep on the top of the tour bus."

"You have got to be kidding me."

"Nope, not kidding."

Clay woke up the next morning to the sound of sirens and bull horns. The bus was surrounded by police cars, fire trucks and ambulances. Oh my God he thought, has there been a fire or something?

Just then he remembered the FBI in his pocket. About the same time a fire truck ladder rose up to the level of the top of the bus and a policeman stared him in the eye.

"Hey there sleepy head." Said the policeman. "We've been looking all over for you."

"Oh, geez man, I'm sorry. I came up here to veg for a while and fell asleep. I'm sorry, I fell asleep looking at the stars."

The voice in his earpiece was going on like a crazy person.

"Ok, ok, it won't happen again."

Clay got down off the top of the bus and thanked everyone for their attention, and apologized for the inconvenience. Oh man, I need a shower and some coffee.

His band mates met him at the lobby; not looking any too happy with him.

"Hey guys, I just needed a few moments to myself in the quiet. I fell asleep accidently. I certainly didn't mean to alarm anyone. That was quite a response though."

Chapter Twenty-Seven

Ahn had searched various ways into Bac's cage. The vents on the roof held some promise. Tonight, she would take a closer look.

Darkness set in and she got a good hook and climbed up to the roof. She found a vent that was a prime candidate for entry. She also found a huge junction box. It was encased in military grade steel; it also looks like it might contain the T-1 trunk line the team was searching for.

Ahn scrambled back down and gathered with the team. The team consisted of experts in communications, explosives, as well as several others for protection of assets. They were equipped with special dart guns to give anyone in the vicinity a long nap. The darts dissolved after placement so there was no injection mark.

The op needs to be clean so all the trouble lands squarely in the lap of the Bac Thu organization. No trace of them must remain following the completion of the program.

Ahn, "Are we ready?"

All the team members used hand signals to show agreement.

"Let's go, on three. One...two...three."

The shooters took down several guards and stayed in place while the specialist climbed to the top of the cage and started working. The explosives specialist set special detonation cord all around the base of the encasement.

It burned through the steel like hot butter. So far so good. Next, they pried the edges to lift the top off of the junction box. The box was extremely heavy. They struggled for a minute but finally managed to move it far enough to expose the extravagant inner workings of the electronics junction. It was a maze of circuit boards and switches.

The communications expert started hooking alligator clips to various parts of the incoming and outgoing circuit boards and started downloading the corrupted software messages to the main frame.

Ahn had to get inside to trigger the keyboard to make the outgoing fraudulent messages connect.

She pried open the vent cover exposing the room below. She hooked her cords to the outside piping and rappelled down. She was about halfway to the floor when she spotted the lone person inside the cage.

A voice spoke from a dark corner. "Hello agent M-3 or can I call you Ahn? I would have thought you would have just come in the front door; all my guards are sleeping. This room was designed to be functional, not a vault. Honestly, I never believed anyone would have the stones to come here. It appears I was wrong about that. I seem to have seriously underestimated the response I would get for chasing after special ops' airmen.

I'm a black-market guru or privateer you might say. I'm not a security expert by any means."

"You're an American. Who are you?"

"Well since we're here about to make history I'll tell you, my story. I was a supply sergeant for the Army some years ago. I was stationed at one of the early fire bases. We were ambushed and I was declared MIA. Actually, I'd snuck off into the forest and waited till the smoke settled.

After a few weeks the fire base was abandoned. The Army left everything but the kitchen sinks behind. I got myself connected with a local black marketer and started swapping out stuff for other stuff and made some big money. The black market already existed, I just decided to make my way in with all sorts of surplus materials left behind and presto, here I am.

The supply train the FAC guys targeted was one of my special equipment caravans full of high-tech sensors and communications devices. Those hi-tech sensors are how I knew every move you've made since you got on the trail pushing a bike. Actually, Ahn, I knew you were here all along. I will confess I didn't know about the new dissolving darts. That's pretty clever.

I know there is a guy on the roof of this building about to sabotage my whole operation. He should know there are some fail safe devices in that box of surprises up there. Just saying. I mean I know your guys are listening so might as well keep them in the loop.

This isn't a spy level operation here. I just wanted to keep the curious out of my hair. I also have a team of my own just out of range ready to sweep you up when I pop a flare stationed on the roof.

So how can I help you, Ahn?"

Ahn rappelled the rest of the way to the floor.

"Actually, I need you to move over a few feet so I can use the keyboard and install my floppy disk. Can you do that for me?"

"Well sure Ahn I can do that, for a price."

"What might that be mister...what did you say your name was?"

"Connors, just call me Jay."

"What's your deal Jay?" Asked Ahn.

"I know this gig is over, what I need is out of here. The guards out there are to keep me in not you out. I'm actually a prisoner here. I trade my life for my procurement expertise.

Go ahead and burn this thing down. Oh, by the way the Cherry-1 guys can relax, nobody is after them anymore. When it first happened, we had to display a show of force to send a message to leave us alone. It worked too. Until it didn't.

Get me out of here. I have all sorts of contacts and supply lines, you name it, it's yours just get me out of here."

"Aren't you afraid of going to jail?" asked Ahn.

"Nah...I'm worth a ton of gold. My part of the deal is my freedom and a place to hide out, you get all my contacts and supply connections. Is it a deal?"

Ahn knew the team was listening in and with a satellite relay so was headquarters. They conferenced really quick and told her to tell him it was a deal. But first hit the "Any key" on the keyboard just to make sure he's not bluffing.

"Ahn said, well Jay it's a deal. Well get you out of here."

She then shot a paint ball at the keyboard and the screen flashed and glowed a dull orange and then turned blue. Jay or whoever he really was, "screamed oh no, nooooo," pounding his fists on the keyboard.

"Good bye Jay or whoever you are."

Ahn climbed up the rope and the team climbed down from the roof, but first they stuffed explosives into the mortar tubes on the roof to prevent any signal flares from shooting out. Just as they hit the ground, they heard several thuds and then the inside of the cage lit up like a roman candle.

The team retreated to a safe location to monitor the situation. Ahn called in to Base.

"Base this BTF -1, how copy?"

"Copy loud and clear BTF-1, what's with the BTF thing anyway," quizzed Base?

"Ah well, I thought since this operation is called "Boil the Frog" we could use some callsigns to go along with that." Said Ahn.

"Catchy," was the response, "what's your status there BTF-1," snickers were heard in the ear pieces.

"Ahn replied, the cage is burning, the high voltage spike delivered a death blow to any electronics inside or close by. The guy inside, whoever he was, didn't appear to escape, but he might have gotten out by the door. When I last saw him, he was frantically trying to revive the equipment, to no avail, I might add."

"Copy," said base, "we had a pretty good idea who the guy was and he was not a hostage. We need for the a...BTF team to hang there for a little while longer until we verify the false messages and account information has changed. Base out."

Ahn said, "ok guys stay on your toes. As soon as we get the all clear we're going to grab one of their vehicles and exfil out of here. There is a main highway just north of here about two klicks, we will catch that and drive on into Thailand."

Operative BTF-4-1 turned to the operative next to him. "The waiting drives me nuts. I'd rather be riding a bucking bronc that sitting around. I feel like I'm blending into the landscape."

Operative BTF-5-1 replied, "Yeah I get you man, I want to go pop somebody, my adrenaline is insane right now."

Operative BTF-6-1 chimed in, "I could use a drink, a smoke, and a nap."

"Base to BTF team. The Yankees have won the pennant, 9 to 0. Repeat the Yankees have won the pennant, 9 to 0. Get out of there, exfil to location Xray, Zulu, alpha, dash-88 for flight out. The Frog is Boiled and served up on a silver platter. Great job everyone. Base out."

Ahn and the rest of Team BTF-1 commandeered a truck, which turned out to be pretty easy. The distractions they had planted had everyone running for cover. It was chaos everywhere, people running and screaming.

They made their way up to highway 6 and headed west to cross the border at Krong Poi Pet, and then into Thailand. They continued west to UDORN AB where they met up with headquarters.

"Nice job everyone, the Bac Thu's organizations competitors will sweep in and take up the pieces. This BTF type of operation is really starting to catch on. There may be many more of these ops, low and slow, 'Gaslighting' them to death."

"You guys go get some hot chow and we will debrief later this afternoon. Ahn, hang back a minute. Just to make sure none of your people are moles for any other organization we're going to quarantine everyone for two weeks to make sure. If there is an 'ADHD mole' in the group their boredom will reveal itself.

Ahn, from here forward you are promoted to section leader first class. Congratulations."

Chapter Twenty-Eight

"Say Bud, I'd like to travel up through the South Dakota badlands and end up at Mount Rushmore. We've got some extra time; don't you think that would be ok?" Asked Clay. "I've never been to that part of the country and since we're about finished with this gig I'd like to see more of the scenery."

"Sure," said Bud, "I should mention it to the guys though, just in case they had some other plans."

RJ thought, we've had a really good run. It's almost a shame that it's over in a couple of weeks.

"Hey guys what do you think about driving up through the South Dakota badland and going to see Mount Rushmore?" Bud asked them.

They all looked at each other and in chorus said, "Sure, that would work out fantastically."

They had spent a good three weeks around Boulder, had a great time, ate some good food met some wonderful people. Had a first-hand experience with the first responders of the local area, thanks to sleepy head Clay.

The other four band mates held an impromptu private conference.

Clay hollered out, "what you guys talking about anyway?" As Bud fired up the engine and the airbrakes hissed. They headed out for the next stop on their journey.

"Awe, nothing, we have a little surprise up our sleeve for you. We heard you like fried chicken and there's a perfect little spot just around Cheyenne. We're gonna stop there and feed you fried chicken till you can crow like a rooster."

The Bus chugged away and merged onto the interstate highway headed to Wyoming. They made good time and got to the Chicken Restaurant just in time for dinner. The group bailed out of the bus and went into the restaurant and found a large table where they could spread out.

After we ordered our food. Ed jumped up and said he needed to use the rest room. On his way back he stopped by a pay phone on the wall next to the bar. He put in some money and waited as the phone rang on the other end of the line. Presumably someone answered as Ed spoke some strange phrase into the receiver. After a few moments he bristled.

"Are you sure?" He repeated, "the Yankees won the pennant 9 to 0. The Yankees won the pennant 9 to 0." He then mumbled a bunch of gibberish into the receiver and hung up.

"Great news guys," he said, "the Yankees have won the pennant 9 to 0. Isn't that great news?" he asked.

I was of course completely baffled as the baseball season wasn't nearly over. I knew Ed was from New York but this was a bit weird. Oh well here comes the chicken. That is some good-looking fried chicken if I don't say so myself. Looks almost as good as the fare at the Lazy J.

The tone and attitude of the group was substantially more upbeat after the fried chicken feed and apparently the news of the Yankees winning the pennant, which still didn't make a lick of sense to me.

They got back on the bus and settled in.

"RJ, kick back and take a nap, the next stop is quite a way off."

What the ... did Ed just call me RJ? I must be imagining things again. I swear a good chicken dinner can make me hallucinate.

The bus chugged away out onto the road, air brakes hissing.

I woke up in a haze after what seemed like hours. It was early daylight and we were stopped on the side of the road next to a burned-out bus, interestingly enough it looked just like this one.

I was sleepy and struggled to sit up. My head trying to clear I looked out the window at the bus across the road. There were three guys spraying the side of the burned-out wreck with machine gun fire. The noise echoing through my groggy brain, I was suddenly wide awake. The bus appeared to have similar markings just like mine, only burned and barely visible. What the heck is going on?

"RJ," said some guy that looked a lot like Ed only he had on a suit and sunglasses. The other two guys looked like Zane and Nick, where was Bud and Piper in all of this. Once again did he just call me RJ?

"Get up, get all your stuff."

I followed his orders and collected my stuff, clothes, guitar, paperwork and stood up.

"Come with me," he said.

He led me to a helicopter waiting about fifty yards away.

"Go there and get in," he said. "I'll explain later."

Once again, I followed orders. I climbed up into the chopper and waited as the crew finished shooting up the bus and then set it on fire again. Bud drove the Jelly Bean away. Another one of the guys drove the pickup. The other guys got into the waiting chopper and we took off. My head was swirling with questions and a wee bit of vertigo.

The chopper landed at an airbase I was unfamiliar with. There was a sign on the roof of a hangar that read Offutt Airbase. Wait isn't that in Nebraska.

The helicopter landed and everyone exited the craft. I was escorted to a sound proof room and told to make myself comfortable. I dropped my stuff on the floor and looked around. There was a pot of coffee over on the table. I poured myself a cup and sat down.

In a few minutes Ed, Nick and Zane came into the room.

Nick said, "We can explain what's going on and answer any of your questions. This room has all the comforts of home so make yourself comfortable. Except you can't go outside...yet."

"I don't even know where to start," said RJ. "Obviously, you know me as RJ, so fill in the blanks for me, will you please."

"You can call us by Ed, Nick, and Zane but that's not our real names. We're special ops and were assigned to your case from the beginning. You have no idea how many threats we eliminated on the way through the country. But and this is a huge BUT. We believe that all the threats are gone. The Yankees winning the pennant 9 to 0 was code for the elimination of the Bac Thu organization. It's over.

You will be in quarantine for the next two weeks to make sure there are no further threats. On the last day, you, your family, Baker and his family, and Cherry will all get to watch a video news program on national TV news, wrapping this case up for good. Any questions?"

"No," said RJ, "I think that about covers it."

Ed, or whatever his name is, continued. "Directly after the video airs on TV, the same day, you will be delivered to the Lazy J. If Miss Wilson so desires, she will be afforded transportation to the Lazy J as well. Keep in mind, she might possibly want to go home or stay where she is, it will be totally up to her at that point.

You will have no contact with the outside world until we can confirm that all threats have been terminated. So, sit back and get comfortable."

Is this really happening, I thought? What does this all mean? I'm going to be free to go home and use my real identity, I can be with Cheery, if she still wants me. I don't have to slink around and look over my shoulder all the time. How about that Ed, Nick, and Zane anyway. They were some pretty cool guys and could definitely play some great music.

I can go back to town and get that little house I dreamed of. Get me a barn and a goat and a cow and might even get a dog and name him Rex. Get some sugar beets and raise them on a patch of ground, get a tractor and a pickup truck. And there's the issue of the Cherry-1 stingray. I wonder where she is?

It's been almost three years since I've seen Cherry, I miss her something awful. The last thing I ever wanted to do was break her heart. I hope she can forgive me over time.

What about Bud and Piper, where did they get off too? I swear, he's an angel.

Chapter Twenty-Nine

The phone rang on the wall at the Lazy J. Martha got up and answered the call.

"Hello," she said.

The voice on the line said, "The Yankees have won the pennant 9 to 0, I repeat the Yankees have won the pennant 9 to 0. More details to follow."

Click, it hung up from the other end.

"That was strange," said Martha. "The caller said the Yankees have won the pennant 9 to 0, like I cared anything about baseball."

Dan about jumped out of his skin.

"Oh my God he yelled, Oh my God, that's the code for the successful end of the Bac Thu operation. That's great news," as he hopped up and down. "This is fantastic."

"Well ok," said Martha. "What does that mean?"

"Well when we were unable to see RJ at Terry Haute that meant the exfil stage of the operation was about to happen. The special ops people were going to make Clay and the Snake Skin Rangers disappear. The next phase was to take RJ to an undisclosed location and quarantine him until they are sure it's all done.

It means that in about two weeks he will come walking through that door as Roy Jansen.

We are to wait for further information. They said to watch the TV news in two weeks, all will be revealed then. Oh, wow this is so fantastic," Dan said, overcome with excitement. He could hardly contain himself.

Martha said, "Well then, I've got a lot of work to do. We must have a grand celebration. I will get his room ready and ... oh my." She burst into tears. "I'm so happy I could cry."

Dan looked at her lovingly and grinned. "I think that's obvious dear."

Chapter Thirty

Agent Renfroe answered the phone. She repeated the phrase, "the Yankees have won the pennant 9 to 0."

"Oh my gosh," she squealed. Dancing like her pants were on fire. Getting Cherry's attention.

"What is it Marsha," she blurted out.

"The Bac Thu organization is gone; they've been taken out."

"What's that mean?" asked Cherry.

"It means there are no more threats to worry about. RJ can come home as RJ and you can join him if you choose. Cherry you will soon be free of this burden and can go anywhere anytime you want. Of course, you can go to be with RJ if you choose. It has been nearly three years after all. You might not feel the same as before. It's your choice to make. The Agency will deliver you anywhere you want to go when the quarantine is over.

We have to wait two weeks to confirm the threats are over for sure. At the end of that time, we are to watch the TV news for a big reveal. Until then we go about our business as usual.

Bless your heart Cherry, you are one of the most resilient people I've ever had the pleasure of knowing. I hope you're happy no matter where you go and what you do."

Cherry thought her heart was going to beat out of her chest. It wasn't her she was worried about, what if RJ after all this time had changed his mind about her. I have to push those thoughts out; I just can't think like that. Positive thoughts Cherry, that's what RJ used to tell her, positive thoughts.

Chapter Thirty-One

The doorbell rang, Sandra, 1st Lt. Baker's wife jumped up and answered the door.

"Gary, there's someone here to see you."

"Who is it?" he asked.

"Ah, come see for yourself."

Gary got up and went to the door.

"Hello," he said, "can I help you?"

"Hello 1st Lt. Baker," the stranger said, "I'm an agent with the Special Ops division of the Airforce.

In two weeks on this date, day and time there will be a nationwide TV broadcast. After that broadcast you will receive a knock at the door. The agent will hand you, Sergeant Jansen and Cherry Wilson a package. Inside that package will be documents that restore your previous identities, a financial package from the proceeds of the drained accounts of the Bac Thu organization, and Military documents showing you are medically discharged from the Military at the rank of Captain, Senior Master Sergeant Jansen to Chief, and Captain Wilson to the rank of Major.

During the next days you will behave as though you know nothing of this. There's still some doubt, a very slight doubt, that the threats are over for good. We are confident that this is over, however we want to make sure, as sure as we can humanly determine.

Financial scans are being run continuously, as well as all points of transportation for any signs of unusual activity.

Stay calm and know this. Special Ops has worked diligently on yours and Sergeant Jansens behalf to bring this to an end. All of the people affected by this interruption will be receiving compensation out of the funds captured from the Bac organizations activities. Including as many of the victims of their reign of evil that we can locate.

Have a good day, Captain Baker."

Sandra looked at Gary, she was absolutely astonished.

"I never thought this day would come, and yet here it is"

"Almost," said Gary. "The next two weeks are going to be a wide range of feelings and emotions. We mustn't get ahead of ourselves. Let's pray that the new beginning has come and our freedom has been secured."

Gary, Sandra and their two children had lived very austere lives over the past few months. They're eager to see family and go outside without fear of being recognized.

As the days began to tick away, their excitement-built day by day.

Cherry wiled away the time walking the halls of the hospital. She couldn't sit still.

Finally, someone asked her if she was ok.

"Oh, I'm fine," she said, "I have a lot on my mind, something is coming up, the waiting is making me crazy. I think I might have to cut back on the caffeine though."

She stayed away from Agent Renfroe absolutely terrified that she might give her bad news before the end of the two weeks. Agent Renfroe kept a watchful eye, but gave her some space.

Dan and Martha stayed busy at the Lazy J; the busyness kept their minds occupied. Occasionally they would exchange glances and chuckle nervously.

RJ was about to lose his mind cooped up in the sound proof room in the hangar. They did let him watch videos on a VHS player. He found some of them interesting and nearly wore out the player.

They brought him a racket ball and he bounced that around till his hands were raw. He got ahold of some paper and pencil and started writing down some of his thoughts over the last few months. This kept him occupied and as it turned out, to be great therapy.

He still had his guitar and strummed the strings when he got nervous, anxious, depressed or just felt like it. He very nearly wore out the snapshot of Cherry and the stingray.

At Special Ops headquarters they are busy monitoring the world-wide situation and planning for any possible situation that might arise. There had been one disturbance but that turned out to be Bac Thu's competition ginning up for an attack on some unsuspecting illegal drug manufacturing operation. The alert raised their attention, putting a BTF team on standby. They ultimately relaxed when the situation became clearer.

In a side note Sergeant Connors, the Bac Thu king pin was spotted in Bangkok working as a fry cook in a Thai restaurant.

The BTF team that took down the Bac Thu organization has also been quarantined. So far there are no moles.

Three days to go. All is well.

Chapter Thirty-Two

Countdown is on, thirty minutes to go. Everyone has been contacted and have access to the TV news. Everyone is ready. Tension is high. Feelings are raw and sensitive. Bring it on…please.

The tones played from the network news. Everyone was on the edge of their seats. The commentator greeted the audience.

"Greetings everyone from New York, New York. We will get straight to some breaking news.

A tour bus for the music group, 'Clay Carter and the Snake Skin Rangers' was found in the badlands of South Dakota yesterday. It was burned out and full of bullet holes. Investigators found no sign of life. The investigation is ongoing but given the scene, they don't hold out much hope. The area is notorious for drug running. Gangs have also been reported operating in the area. A spokesperson for the 'Rangers' refused to comment, appearing overcome with emotion."

Cherry, Dan and Martha, RJ, the Bakers, they all gasped as the news hit them.

Agent Renfroe grabbed Cherry and said, "Keep watching."

Dan held Martha and told her, "Keep watching."

RJ was dazed and confused but the agent that just entered the room, said, "Keep watching."

Just then the commentator announced, "In other news, two airmen presumed lost in the jungles of Panama came walking out of the wood on their own power yesterday. They are a bit malnourished and looked a complete mess but are ecstatic to be back to civilization. They gave a brief interview thanking the locals that had helped them and wishing their families back home love and kisses. They will be stateside by the end of the week, where they will be greeted by a medical team for evaluation and then released to travel. Welcome home guys.

And that's our news for today."

The Bakers are beside themselves with joy.

Cherry squealed and danced around the room. "Oh my God what does this mean?" she asked Renfroe.

"It means you can go and do whatever you want starting right now."

Cherry replied, "I have some affairs to tie up here and I'm off to the Lazy J. I just hope RJ still wants me?"

Renfroe mumbled under her breath, "I don't think that's going to be a problem."

Dan and Martha danced around and laughed out loud. The atmosphere had changed significantly. Customers are watching with great interest as the raucous laughter raged on.

RJ turned to the agent in the room. "Now what?

He replied, "Get your stuff. There is a helicopter waiting on the apron to take you home."

Two hours later. RJ opened the door to the Lazy J. He staggered in and dropped his stuff on the floor. The room exploded with cheers and applause. Confetti flying everywhere and banners welcoming him home. They all burst into tears of joy. Hugs and kisses all around.

Tom had made it home and Lanora was there with her family. One of her kids asked her, "Momma...who's that?"

Lanora laughed and told her, "That's my brother, your uncle Roy."

The crowd settled down and everyone came by and congratulated Roy on his safe return. Common question was, "How was life in the Jungle?"

His common reply was, "It was hot, wet, and sticky, full of bugs and snakes. I'm so glad to be back on dry land."

The next day after all the excitement had died down, he sat across from his dad and mom at one of the dining tables.

"So, what's next mom and dad?" he asked.

"Well son," said Dan, "just take it easy for a few days, take some time to gather your thoughts and put a plan together."

"Has anyone heard from Cherry? I have so many questions. Will she still want me. Will she be the same, will I be the same."

Martha answered that question, "None of us are the same Roy, what we need to know is are we all on the same team heading in the best direction for our lives. Cherry will let you know soon enough what her feelings are."

"I've waited, we've all waited for this moment. I don't want to mess it up."

The next day RJ woke up in a different world. One he hadn't seen in years. It was awkward and yet comforting at the same time. He got up, dressed and went over to the Lazy J for breakfast.

"This is a really good cup of coffee," he told the fry cook and the waitress serving him.

He sat there at the bar wondering what he might do this day. Suddenly he thought he heard a familiar sound, nah it can't be, that sounds just like the stingray. He whirled around and looked out the window. He didn't see anything; the sound had stopped.

I must be imaging things today he mused.

He heard the bell on the door as it opened, like it does dozens of times a day. He heard footsteps coming up behind him. The hair stood up on the back of his neck. Suddenly he smelled the most fragrant perfume.

A voice behind him spoke, "What did you do to your hair?"

He whirled around knocking the coffee cup to the floor.

"Oh my God, it's you, Cotton Top, it's really you."

They held onto each other as if one of them might get away.

There was a giant roar of applause from the back of the kitchen.

He backed away, still holding her hands. "Let me look at you. Oh my God you're a sight for sore eyes. How have you been, how are you here, I think my chest is going to explode."

Cherry, wiped away her own tears of joy. "Roy Jansen, you have taken us all on quite a journey. It's time to change lanes and move on buster. I've missed you so much and we have so much to catch up on. I'm here for as long as you want me."

Roy got down on one knee, right there on the spot and said, "Cherry Wilson will you marry me?"

She grabbed him and smothered him with kisses and squealed a happy, "YES SIR, I will."

The room erupted in another giant round of applause as Dan and Martha came rushing in from the back room.

Thus started a new life, a new beginning.

Chapter Thirty-Three

Martha and Cherry's mother Deb, planned a wedding fit for royalty. There would be about fifty guests and they would use their little church as the venue for the nuptials and the reception would be at the Lazy J. They arranged for the flowers, food, and other necessities.

RJ and Cherry wanted to keep it lowkey and maybe even just do a Justice of the Peace thing. "Oh no, that was not going to happen, steamed the mothers. "We're going to have a proper wedding celebration. You owe us that much." RJ and Cherry somewhat reluctantly agreed.

And then the word got out. At first the guest list swelled to one hundred or so. A couple of days later it doubled again to over two hundred fifty.

"Oh my," said Martha, "this is beyond our capacity. We need help."

Again, the word got out and resources multiplied. Someone arranged for a larger church in another town close by. Food caterers lined up to bid for the business. And just when everyone thought ok, we have a handle on this affair. The word got out again that the celebration had moved to a larger location, and the guest list shot up like a fireworks display.

People from all over the country wanted in on the celebration of the century. Someone arranged for the wedding to occur in a sports stadium with a forty thousand seat capacity. The venue would offer food for sale. There would still be a small reception with family and close friends at the Lazy J.

Deb and Martha are in over their heads, but they managed to get their skills to rise to the occasion. They would print invitations available at the doors. There would be cupcakes served at the stadium along with a variety of soft drinks. They worried over the cost of the event when community members kicked in with enough money to not only pay for the event but to send the couple on a nice honey moon.

Exhausted the mothers sat down for a coffee.

"Forty thousand cupcakes," sighed Martha, "every bakery in three counties is going to be busy on that chore."

"Did you ever imagine such a thing?" Deb asked Martha.

"No never," she said, "then again, I've heard from people all over the country about how Cherry had changed their lives with her kindness and gentle care in the hospitals she served in. And RJ, he has a squadron of people that has expressed their gratitude at saving their lives as downed aircrew. The both of them have touched so many people in so many ways. It's no shock that there might be a few that would want to honor them. This however, is beyond my wildest dreams. Even special ops have sent in a team for security and to help manage crowd control. I'm absolutely blown away."

"Speaking of those two, where are they today," asked Deb.

"I thought I heard them discussing looking at a little farm house just over the other side of the road. Roy has had his eye on it for a long time. I think the owner might be ready to sell. He hasn't used it in years."

Cherry and RJ pulled up in the driveway of the house. They met with the owner inside and he gave them a tour. Afterward they sat down and discussed terms.

"We'll get back to you by the end of the week," RJ told the owner. "We have to talk financing with our banker."

They went back to the Lazy J and sat down with some paperwork and a cup of coffee.

"What are your thoughts, Cherry?" asked RJ.

"Well, the property will need some renovation and the land some clean up, but I think it will work for us. It's close to everything we want and need. I can work at the local hospital and you can work at the electronics factory. When our kids come along, we will be close to the schools. Do we have enough money to buy it outright?"

"Yes, we do, with what we received from the packages; what I saved from overseas work and never spending a dime. Spending a couple of months in the jungle didn't cost me anything. The music adventure made a lot more money than I imagined and the band mates didn't take a dime since they were on special ops salary the whole time. So yes, we can afford it. We can also afford for you to go back to school and become a doctor if you choose. I would like to get my engineering degree."

"It's done then," said Cherry.

The day after the wedding and right before we take off on our honeymoon, we will complete the paperwork as husband and wife.

They called the owner back and made him an offer which he accepted. They told him as soon as they get married, they would have their lawyer draw up the required paperwork. He agreed verbally, the deal was done.

Cherry giggled, "I have so many ideas to spruce up the place, this will be so much fun. Imagine a place of our own, I can hardly wait."

RJ just smiled; he'd learned not to get in the way of a woman determined.

Tom has flown in and will be the best man. Cherry asked Agent Marsha Renfroe to be her maid of honor, which she gladly accepted. The two of them agreed they are going to keep the attendants to a minimum, at least that would be something they could handle.

Cherry picked a beautiful white gown with a flowing train. RJ went with a tuxedo and a cherry red Cummerbund. Renfroe wore a modest yellow frock, Tom wore a light-yellow tuxedo with white accents. The flowers are white and yellow to match the outfits, except RJ insisted on a bunch of cherry red roses on either side of the podium.

The day was upon them. The bride and groom are away getting dressed while the crowd filled the stadium. Everyone was playing their part perfectly. Music was playing from of all things, a full orchestra.

Dan looked at Joe, Cherry's father and commented, "Quite a shindig we're having today eh." Joe looked absolutely terrified at the thought of walking his daughter down an aisle that was over 100 yards long. What if he tripped or just passed out. He didn't have much longer to think about it as Cherry emerged from the dressing room looking like an absolute angel. Joe gasped for air as his eyes filled with tears.

"Come on my angel," he said to Cherry, "let's go wow the crowd."

The music played; the crowd hushed as they started down the aisle towards the podium. The flower girls splayed their petals and drew giggles from the crowd as they danced down the aisle.

RJ, Tom, Marsha, and the preacher watched in absolute amazement as they approached the podium.

The pair reached the podium and the preacher announced "Who gives this bride?"

Joe stammered out, "Her mother and I do."

Cherry joined the party and the preacher proceeded with the nuptials; the couple shared some of their own vows. The preacher asked for the rings to be presented, first Tom, and then Marsha, Cherry nearly fumbled the catch but swiftly recovered.

"I present to you, Mr. and Mrs. Roy Jansen,"

There was a huge round of applause from the crowd.

"You may now kiss the bride," announced the preacher.

RJ lifted the veil over Cherry's face, and gently kissed her lips.

That was just about the time a flight of F-4 Phantom jets from the Thunderbirds air demonstration team flew over the stadium, much to the delight of the crowd. A lone O-1 circled gently over the stadium.

It was total pandemonium as the couple retreated to a designated location to greet as many of the visitors as possible.

As the crowd dwindled, RJ found the senior special ops agent.

"Hey, how in the world did you pull all of this off?

The agent smiled and said, "Divine Magic."

Cherry and RJ met at the Lazy J for a final reception and send off. There are still a couple of hundred people wanting to see them off.

They made short work of the reception and found the CHERRY-1 stingray all decked out with just married signs all over it. RJ twisted the key in the ignition for the first time in over two years. The engine sprang to life and the pipes started singing a familiar tune. The couple slowly drove out of the parking lot and onto the highway. An entourage of a couple dozen cars shot out after them.

After a few miles they dropped off as they cruised to a nice hotel in a neighboring town.

After unloading luggage, they went to their room, both of them collapsing on the giant bed and fell fast asleep.

The next morning, they were greeted by a tray of tasty treats for breakfast. RJ picked up the newspaper only to find that they were front page news.

"Uh oh," he said, "look at this," he showed Cherry the article.

She perused it and finally said, "Well as least they got my good side."

RJ laughed hysterically, "Oh my God woman, you don't have one...good side, you have a whole group of them.

They finished breakfast and went down to the indoor pool for some exercise and to just chill for a while.

They were drying off when RJ looked at Cherry.

"Sweetheart, I have a proposition for you."

She looked up at him curiously. "What." She asked.

"This hotel stay is not our real honeymoon, it's just a day to clear our heads and think about what we want to do next."

"Ok," she said, "what's on your mind."

"Next week is Veterans Day, there are some people in Springfield Missouri that are dying to meet you. They even promised me that they would put on a parade just for you if they ever got the chance. I intend to give them that chance. We can drive up to Springfield and meet with the group there. On Veterans Day you will get your parade and them the opportunity to honor you, the way they would love too. There are many of the vets there that you treated in hospital while you were overseas. They want to thank you. After the parade we can go anywhere you want. A beach in Florida or California, or where ever your heart desires. As long as it's with me I don't care. What do you say?"

"Well, since you put it like that, let's go. I was thinking maybe a beach in Florida and a trip to the new giant amusement park there. That would be fun. Then we can come home and start work on our home. Ooooo, I'm so excited."

They caught Route 66 and made their way to Springfield. They got a room and checked in. The proprietor recognized them instantly and told them their money was no good there. He gave them the best room in the hotel, they gladly accepted.

The next day we drove over the Vet center and I walked in. "Hey there Terry, do you remember me"

"Sort of, I think your name is Clay maybe," she looked curiously at him.

"Well, the real me is Roy Jansen and I need to talk to Roger about that parade he was going to put on. Is he around?"

"Sure," she said, "he's around the corner drinking coffee with some of the guys, they're planning the float for the Veterans Day parade in a couple of days from now."

"Thanks, I'll see myself around. Roger, long time no see, how's it going?"

Roger stood up with an astonished look on his face. "You, you're that guy, the CHERRY-1 guy, isn't your name Clay or something?"

"Well, you're right, I'm the guy, but my name is Chief Master Sergeant Roy Jansen, I have with me Major Cherry Jansen, my new bride. I promised you a couple of years ago if I got the chance, I would bring her here and you could give her a parade. Well guys, she's with me here. When and where is that parade?

The group fell all over themselves at the news.

"Why yes, we're just now planning the parade for Veterans Day, she could actually be the Queen of the parade. Where is she, can we meet her?"

"She's waiting in the car. I'll go get her."

Cherry got out of the car and we went in to meet the group. She stopped and caught her breath.

"I recognize you," she told Roger, "How are you getting on?" she said.

"I'm fine, thanks to you and your fellow medical professionals. There are several of the guys here that you helped get back home. We are so grateful that you're here."

They shared a meal that evening and told stories of how they got there and how their journey to healing had progressed.

Cherry and many other medical professionals performed miracles on seriously damaged bodies to restore their spirits and heal their wounds.

"And you RJ," said Roger, "how many lives you and your fellow FAC crew saved. There are a few of them here eager to show their gratitude as well."

"We plan to be in the parade and then, we're heading off to our honeymoon," said RJ.

The Veterans Day parade was quite the affair in Springfield. They followed the parade route, smiling and waving to the crowd. They shook hands with many a grateful solder, sailor, marine, and airman, and their families.

"Roger, it's been a pleasure, we're taking off now. God bless you guys and your mission here."

The couple arrived in Florida and stayed in a motel on the beach between Ft Walton and Panama City. The sand was like talcum powder it was so fine. They then traveled over to the new amusement park; it was the size of a small city.

They then set their sights for home. While driving along the coast RJ made a proposal.

"I'm thinking about trading this old crate in on a pickup truck, what do you think," he asked?

"Don't you dare she squealed, are you crazy!" While whacking him over the head with a map.

"I was joking, it was just a joke, I was kidding," while defending himself from the weaponized map.

"Hey did we just have our first fight, cool, did I win?"

"Not hardly buster," she said grinning a huge smile.

Upon arriving RJ parked the car and opened the front door. He grabbed Cherry up and carried her across the threshold.

When he set her down, she was astonished at the state of the house. While they were gone several local craftspeople took her ideas and put every single one of them in place. She ran around overflowing with joy.

"Oh RJ, it's just so amazing."

Chapter Thirty-Four

It was a couple of years later, Cherry had finished her Doctorate and RJ had his engineering degree. Cherry was working in a clinic for children that she had established. RJ was working at the electronics factory and was developing all manner of Laser devices from measurement to entertainment. He was especially proud of his holographic lasers used by music groups everywhere. He also worked on Cold lasers for medical treatment, those are having a profound effect on pain management.

RJ was sitting in the Lazy J having a morning cup of coffee. Martha and Deb were playing with young Douglas, the new addition to the Jansen family. Cherry was busy that day with clinic responsibilities, she would meet them for lunch a little later.

Just then there was a glint of something very polished. It was a bus that had just pulled into the Truckstop across the highway, it looked like of all things, the Jelly Bean. His curiosity got the best of him. He got up and started for the door.

"Where are you going," quizzed Martha sternly, "Cherry will be here any minute."

"I'll be right back," said RJ, as he exited the door.

He walked quickly across the parking lot and stared in amazement at the bus. It had the words, "Bud Conley and the Snake Skin Rangers" painted on the side of the bus.

All RJ could think of was, what ... the.

He made his way around the end of the bus and spied a figure pumping fuel. He walked up and leaned on the side of the bus.

"I know who you are, he said, you're that rock star that disappeared a couple years ago. They say he went underground to escape attention. What's it going to take for me to keep your secret, huh?

Turning slowly around, "Is that so," he said. "Well how much would it take for you to keep my secret. Fifty, a hundred?"

"I said, I could really use a new pair of tennis shoes."

Bud laughed and smiled; When he smiled, I swear his whole face sparkled like an explosion of confetti.

Epilogue

Cherish our nations veterans both combat and noncombat, women and men who have stepped up and done their duty to their country. Otherwise, we might be owing allegiance to those who don't have our best interest in mind.

If you're in the Washinton D.C. area please visit the Women in Vietnam memorial on the National Mall.

There are several FAC memorials in the United States honoring the several hundreds of airmen that gave their all, in service to their country, one of which is located at Hurlburt field in Ft. Walton Beach Florida.

"He shall call upon me, and I will answer him: I will be with him in trouble; I will deliver him, and honor him." Psalms 91:15

www.ingramcontent.com/pod-product-compliance
Lightning Source LLC
Chambersburg PA
CBHW061452150726

47987CB00001B/421